THE FABULOUS FIVE

Class Trip Calamity

BETSY HAYNES

A BANTAM SKYLARK BOOK®
NEW YORK · TORONTO · LONDON · SYDNEY · AUCKLAND

RL 5, 009–012

CLASS TRIP CALAMITY
A Bantam Skylark Book / June 1992

ISBN 0-553-15969-0

Published simultaneously in the United States and Canada

*Bantam Books are published by Bantam Books, a division of Bantam Doubleday
Dell Publishing Group, Inc. Its trademark, consisting of the words "Bantam
Books" and the portrayal of a rooster, is Registered in U.S. Patent and Trade-
mark Office and in other countries. Marca Registrada. Bantam Books, 666
Fifth Avenue, New York, New York 10103.*

PRINTED IN THE UNITED STATES OF AMERICA
CWO   0 9 8 7 6 5 4 3 2 1

IT WAS SUPPOSED TO BE
THE BEST TIME OF THE YEAR. . . .

"Hey, this is the last time we'll be able to sing 'Go! Fight! Win! Wakeman Junior High!'" said Curtis when the singing died down. "From now on it will be Wakeman Middle School."

"Right!" yelled Derek Travelstead. "Let's sing it again!"

"Same song, second verse, a little bit louder, and a little bit worse," chanted Laura and Tammy.

By about the twelfth chorus, Jana started to relax. Nobody really had the nerve to bring booze on this bus, much less drink it, she decided.

She whispered her feeling to Randy, adding, "Why would anyone want to spoil such a good time by doing something like that, anyway?"

Before Randy could respond, Jana saw Tammy turn to Melissa McConnell, who was sitting across the aisle from her. "It's time to bring out the thermoses," Tammy whispered. "Pass it on."

CHAPTER

1

*B*umpers was jammed with kids from Wakeman Junior High on Friday night after the movie when Jana Morgan and her best friends pushed their way through the fast-food restaurant. Booths and bumper cars were overflowing with boys and girls, and the line at the order counter reached almost to the front door.

"Wow! Have you ever seen such a crowd in your life?" Beth Barry shouted over the noise.

Katie Shannon pointed toward the far end of the counter. "Look. Mr. Matson's even brought in a television set so we can watch the news report."

"Oh, my gosh!" said Melanie Edwards. "I'm so nervous. What if it doesn't pass?"

"We've all got our fingers crossed," Jana assured her.

1

Katie laughed. "Right. I'll bet there are more fingers crossed in this room than in anyplace else in America."

"Or the world!" added Beth with a dramatic sweep of her hand.

"Quick. There's an empty bumper car!" shouted Jana. She made a beeline toward a red bumper car that three eighth-grade boys were vacating. "Let's grab it!"

The four girls had barely settled into the car when a cheer went up in the crowd. Glancing around, Jana saw that Mr. Matson had turned on the television set and was flipping through the channels with his remote control, finally stopping at channel 30, the local station.

"Shhh! Everybody quiet!"

"Yeah, pipe down, everybody! It's time."

The crowd grew quiet as the channel 30 theme music came on and the camera zoomed in on Marge Whitworth at the news desk.

"Good evening, everyone. This is Marge Whitworth with the ten-o'clock news. Our top story tonight concerns the school board's nearly unanimous vote just moments ago to change Wakeman Junior High into a middle school. The change will take place at the beginning of the next school year, in September, and will also include enlarging the high school to include ninth-graders. The change was brought about by overcrowding—"

Pandemonium broke out as all the kids in the place scrambled to their feet, clapping and stamping and shouting at the top of their lungs. Dozens of drinking-straw wrappers streaked into the air like rockets.

Jana hugged Beth, Katie, and Melanie. She couldn't remember when she had been so excited. Across the room she could see Randy Kirwan, her steady boy-friend, and she gave him a thumbs-up sign.

Dekeisha Adams perched on the edge of the red bumper car as the noise began to subside. "Whew! I can't believe it," she said, shaking her head and grin-ning at the same time. "Do you realize that when they change Wakeman from a junior high with seventh, eighth, and ninth grades to a middle school with sixth, seventh, and eighth grades, we'll be the *upperclassmen* next year!"

"Yeah," said Katie. "What a switch, huh? We'll go from being the youngest—'seventh-grade babies' they called us this year, in case you've forgotten—to the oldest and the biggest deals on campus, the eighth-graders."

"And just think what a great homecoming it will be for Christie," said Jana. "She'll be getting back from London just before school starts." The fifth member of The Fabulous Five, Christie Winchell, had moved to London when her father got a big promotion midway through the school year. But now, much to everyone's relief, the family was moving back again.

"I can't wait to tell her the good news," said Melanie. "I'm going to write her tomorrow."

Beth jumped into the middle of the floor and motioned to Melanie and Dekeisha to join her. "Come on, guys. Let's make up a cheer!"

Laughing, Melanie and Dekeisha raced to Beth. They whispered together for a couple of minutes and then all three stood with their feet wide apart and their hands in the air. Then Melanie and Dekeisha watched for Beth to lead them as they all three chanted:

> *Hey! Hey! What can we say?*
> *We won't be the babies for one more day!*
> *Instead we'll be*
> *the biggest and the best!*
> *Yea! Yea! For Wakeman Middle School!*
> *We de-SERVE it!*

There was another round of wild applause as the rest of the cheerleading squad joined in, and for the next ten minutes Bumpers rocked with the new cheer. Finally, when everyone was near collapse from excitement and exhaustion, Jana and her friends sank back in their red bumper car and took deep swallows of their soft drinks.

"I don't know what you girls are celebrating," said a deep voice from behind the bumper car.

Melanie sat up abruptly, and when Tim Riggs appeared from behind them, she demanded, "What do you mean by that?"

"We eighth-graders are the ones with something to

celebrate," he said, his eyes gleaming. "I mean, the way things were before, we were going into the ninth grade next year, but we would still be in junior high. Now we're going into high school."

Melanie grinned slyly. "Yeah, but you're going to be a freshman—one of the *babies* of the high school. We're going to be the most mature students in our school."

Tim chuckled good-naturedly. "Good point."

"It's too bad that Tim won't be back at Wakeman next year," she said, watching him move on to another group of kids. "I never really noticed how cute he is before."

"Melanie," Katie replied indignantly. "You've got Shane Arrington. What more do you want?"

Melanie frowned and opened her mouth to respond, but before she could say a word, Shawnie Pendergast raced up to the bumper car, leaning against it as she tried to catch her breath.

"I just called my parents, and they said I could have a party tomorrow night to celebrate Wacko's becoming a middle school and school's being out in a week and a half!" she said, panting. "You guys can come, can't you?"

"Gosh, I'd love to," answered Jana. "I'll have to check with my parents, but I'm sure they'll let me."

"Me, too. Me, too," echoed the others.

"Terrific. I'll talk to you later. I have to ask a bunch more kids." Shawnie whirled away to a nearby booth, where Dekeisha, Alexis Duvall, Lisa Snow, and Marcie Bee were sitting.

Jana sat back, sipping on her soft drink. "You know," she mused, "not only is school almost out for the summer, but there are a lot of great things about to happen."

"Right," said Beth. "Next weekend is the class trip to New York City to visit the Statue of Liberty and Ellis Island."

"Shawnie's having a party tomorrow night," added Melanie.

"And don't forget that Christie is coming home," said Katie.

"And Wakeman Junior High is going to be Wakeman Middle School!" the four friends said in unison and clinked their glasses together in a toast to all the good things to come.

CHAPTER

2

*E*xcept for the fact that there were no bumper cars, Shawnie's basement playroom bore a remarkable resemblance to Bumpers the night before, Jana decided as she skipped down the stairs and entered the room. Mainly because kids were everywhere. At one end of the enormous room a sofa and two love seats formed a semicircle around a huge stone fireplace. The sofa and love seats were loaded with talking, laughing, seventh-grade girls. Laura McCall had the rest of The Fantastic Foursome—Tammy Lucero, Melissa McConnell, and Funny Hawthorne—gathered around her on the sofa, and Jana knew every single girl on the love seats, too.

At the other end of the room the mirrored bar held trays of refreshments, and a group of boys, including

Randy, Scott Daly, Keith Masterson, and Tony Sanchez, were standing around munching brownies. Almost every inch of floor space in between was taken up with couples dancing to rock music or clusters of kids simply standing around talking.

"Now this is what I call a party!" exclaimed Beth, coming up beside Jana and snapping her fingers to the beat. Then she twirled around to show off the crocheted red tunic she was wearing over a bodysuit with a multicolored geometric design. "Like my out-fit?" She ran a hand down the lacy tunic. "I crocheted this myself."

Jana nodded happily. "It's wild. And speaking of wild, isn't this house incredible? I knew it was big, but I never dreamed that Shawnie's playroom was almost the size of a gymnasium."

"Me, either," said Beth. "This must be how the other half lives."

By this time Katie and Melanie had arrived and had stopped to talk to Kimm Taylor before moving on through the crowd toward Jana and Beth.

"Kimm wanted to know what we're going to wear on the trip Saturday," Melanie told them. "I said probably shorts, since it's gotten so warm lately."

"It's going to be a great trip," said Katie. "Mr. Naset has been telling our history class all about Ellis Island and how it was the place where all immigrants to the

United States used to have to stop to get checked out before they entered the country."

"Yeah," added Melanie, "and it's going to be a blast to ride school buses into New York City and then take the ferryboat across New York Harbor. I can't wait."

Katie gave her a dirty look. "Can't you ever be serious? We're going to see an important piece of American history, and all you can think about is riding a bus and a boat."

"I'm looking forward to going out to the Statue of Liberty again," said Jana. "I haven't been there since I was a little girl."

Katie raised her chin and beamed at them. "And doesn't it make you feel proud to know that the Statue welcoming the tired, the poor, the huddled masses to this great country is a woman?"

"Yes, Katie," they mumbled. Then Jana said, "I'll be right back. I want to talk to Randy for a minute."

Jana was glad to escape another scene between Melanie and Katie, and she ducked through the groups of boys and girls to the refreshments, where Randy was standing with his back to her. She tapped him on the shoulder, and when he turned around, she gave him a big smile and said, "So, what do you think of the big news that Wakeman is going to become a middle school?"

Before Randy could answer, Clarence Marshall

reached between them and grabbed a handful of chips, stuffing them in his mouth and speaking at the same time.

"It's great! That's going to make our class BDOCs. *Big deals on campus!*" Laughing at his own joke, Clarence grabbed another handful of chips and turned to some boys standing nearby. "Did you hear that? We're going to be BDOCs next year!"

Jana rolled her eyes. "Riiiight," she said, and Randy chuckled.

Just then she heard a commotion on the stairs and looked up to see Shawnie leading her parents down the steps. Each of them carried four or five big pizza boxes, which they deposited on the bar near the brownies and chips.

A big cheer went up, and Shawnie tossed her blond hair away from her face and held up her hand for quiet. "Okay, everybody. These are my parents."

There was a small ripple of applause, and from somewhere in the back of the crowd came a soft boo.

Shawnie laughed and held up her hand again. "The good news is: Now you see them, and now you don't. They've promised to stay upstairs—*out of sight*—for the rest of the evening!"

This time the cheer was even bigger, and Mr. and Mrs. Pendergast waved to the crowd and made their way back up the stairs.

The music blasted again, pizza boxes flew open, and

the seventh-graders began partying in earnest. Jana was having a terrific time dancing with Randy, eating pizza and brownies, and drinking soda. Yet in spite of all the food and music, all anyone could seem to talk about was the change in Wakeman and the new status it would bring to their class.

"Hey, everybody! We need a toast!" yelled Richie Corrierro. He was standing on a footstool, waving his soda can in the air.

"Yeah!" shouted kids all around the room. "A toast! A toast!"

"Curtis Trowbridge should make it," cried Jana. "He's the president of our class."

"Oh, no," said Shawnie. "Curtis couldn't come tonight."

"Hey, I'll make the toast," called Clarence, and before anyone could object he had climbed on the footstool Richie had been standing on and raised his soft-drink can into the air. "Here's to next year's eighth-graders at Wacko Middle School—the big deals on campus!"

"Yea! Yea!" screamed Jana, jumping up and down and clunking her soda can against Randy's. "Wacko Middle School!"

All around them kids were touching soda cans and cheering.

"Hey, what we really need for our toast is champagne!" called out Joel Murphy.

"Right on," yelled Tony Sanchez. "Hey, Shawnie, there's got to be some champagne in there." He was pointing toward the beautiful mirrored bar, which was littered with empty pizza boxes and brownie crumbs.

"Champagne! Champagne!" A slow chant started at one end of the room and gradually grew. "Champagne! Champagne!"

Shawnie tried desperately to shush the crowd. "My parents are upstairs!" she warned. "Don't let them hear you."

As the crowd grew quieter, Tony Sanchez approached Shawnie. "Hey, we've got to have something for a *real* toast. They even do it on TV."

"Right," said Bill Soliday. "Have you watched those locker room scenes after the World Series and the Super Bowl? Everybody's celebrating like crazy, drinking champagne and pouring it over each other's heads." Grabbing a can of root beer out of Tony's hand, he sloshed some over Tony's head.

The crowd started to get wild again as Tony grabbed for Bill's soda to retaliate.

Jana watched it all in astonishment. Tony and Bill actually sounded serious about toasting with champagne. She turned to say something to the rest of The Fabulous Five, but Katie was already talking.

"Get serious, you guys," Katie yelled to Bill and Tony. "What's the matter with you, anyway? We don't need alcohol. We were already having a good time without it."

"Besides, we don't want to get Shawnie in trouble," Jana chimed in.

Shawnie threw them a look of gratitude. "I'd be grounded for life if I sneaked anything out of my parents' bar and they found out about it."

Soft clucking sounds came from all sides of the room.

"I am not a chicken!" Shawnie said defiantly, but Jana could hear uncertainty creeping into her voice. "I just don't want to get in trouble, that's all."

"Come on, Shawnie," coaxed Joel. "They're not going to find out."

"Yeah. How are they going to know if none of us tells them?" asked Clarence.

"I'd do it if we were at my house," announced Laura McCall. She was leaning against the bar, smiling confidently. "Of course, even if my dad found out, I could twist him around my little finger in a minute. He'd never punish me."

Conversation began buzzing, and Jana pulled Beth closer and whispered, "There she goes again, bragging about how her dad gives her anything she wants to make up for her mother's leaving home when she was little. Half the girls in Wacko are dying to trade places with her."

Beth shrugged. "More than half, if you ask me. But to tell you the truth, I get sick of all her bragging. If things are really that great, why does she have to talk about it all the time?"

"She just likes to make other kids jealous, I guess," Jana replied.

Jana watched as more kids stepped forward, putting pressure on Shawnie. What was most amazing to Jana was that some of the kids were girls whom she considered good friends.

"Just one little toast," said Alexis. "What harm would that do?"

"Right," agreed Sara Sawyer. "I mean, how often do we get to be the big deals on campus?"

"Come on, Shawnie," urged kids from all around the room. "One toast won't hurt."

"I think we should try to stop this," said Jana.

"Don't be a party pooper, Jana," replied Beth, looking thoroughly disgusted. "They're right. One little toast won't hurt. Sometimes I think you're just too serious."

"It would be fun," admitted Melanie. "I've never tasted champagne."

"But, *guys*!" Jana insisted.

Before Jana could come up with another argument, Shawnie had produced a tall, dark green bottle from under the bar. She held it up cautiously and put her finger to her lips. "I can only sneak one bottle of wine from the very back of the cabinet and be sure they won't miss is. And there's just enough for one little sip apiece," she cautioned.

Beth gave Jana another wide-eyed look and said, "Come on, get into the spirit of things. It's just one teensy little toast."

Jana looked around at the excited faces as kids scrambled for paper cups, and a small thrill raced up her back. Maybe she was being a party pooper, after all. Besides, it wasn't much fun being on the outside and watching everybody else have a good time. Beth was right, she decided. How could one teensy little sip hurt anything?

CHAPTER

3

"*M*an, this is cool!" shouted Richie Corrierro as Shawnie opened the bottle of wine and began pouring a small amount in everyone's paper cup.

"Yeah, cool!" shouted Clarence, and several others echoed his words.

Jana watched as Shawnie made her way around the room. Most kids were holding their cups out to her when she came near. Only a few didn't, and she couldn't see Randy well enough to know if he did or not because too many kids were in the way.

"None for me," said Katie when Shawnie approached The Fabulous Five. "I want to stay in complete control of myself."

16

Shawnie shrugged and started to pour wine in Melanie's cup, but Katie wasn't finished talking yet.

"I think you just brought out the booze to get everyone to make fools of themselves."

"Lighten up, Katie," grumbled Beth. "It's just one little sip."

"Right," murmured a few others. "This is fun."

Shawnie pretended not to hear as she continued filling paper cups. Katie frowned, but she didn't say any more.

Jana looked down at the pale liquid in her cup and tried not to grin. As much as she knew she shouldn't be doing this, she couldn't resist feeling sneaky and a little brave. It was fun. And wasn't everybody else doing it, too? Except for Katie, of course, but Katie loved to be different.

"Who's going to make the toast?" asked Tammy Lucero.

"I will!" shouted Clarence, jumping back onto the footstool and almost spilling his wine.

"Not *you* again," said Dekeisha. "I think our toast should be the new cheer Beth made up last night at Bumpers."

"Hey, that's perfect," said Alexis. "Go on, Beth."

Beth bowed theatrically as boys and girls moved aside, clearing a spot for her in the center of the room. Then she handed her paper cup to Alexis and raised her arms into the air and shouted:

Hey! Hey! What can we say?
We won't be the babies for one more day!
Instead we'll be
the biggest and the best!
Yea! Yea! For Wakeman Middle School!
We de-SERVE *it!*

There was a quick gulp as everyone downed the wine, and then the cheering began again. Jana started to cheer, but her throat burned, and she made a face instead. What an awful taste! she thought. How can anyone really like this stuff?

Feeling a tap on her arm, Jana looked around to see Melanie holding out her cup.

"Do you want mine?" Melanie asked barely above a whisper.

Jana shook her head. "Are you kidding? It tastes terrible. But what's the matter? I thought you were dying to try it."

"I was, but . . ." Melanie hesitated, looking around to make sure no one else was listening. "I started to drink it, and then I remembered how one little goof can cause so much trouble."

"What do you mean?" asked Jana.

"Super kisser," Melanie said solemnly.

"Oh, yeah." Jana sighed. "I see what you mean." It was no wonder Melanie had chickened out, she thought. Melanie had believed that a couple of little kisses after The New Generation's rock concert wouldn't hurt anything, either. And boy, had she been wrong. But that was different. How could one little sip of wine hurt? Jana blinked, remembering what her own father's drinking had meant to their family, but she pushed that memory out of her mind. She didn't want to think about that right now. Besides, the party was getting lively again.

"*BDOCs!*" shouted Clarence, wadding up his cup and throwing it into the fireplace. A shower of cups followed his.

Someone had turned the music back on, and a few kids had started to dance again. Beth was standing beside Jana, and she started snapping her fingers to the beat and humming along. "Wow," she said, "this party is a blast now that everybody has loosened up."

The next thing Jana knew, Beth had moved away from her friends. "I think I'll have another little drinky poo," she called out, slurring her words and pretending to be drunk.

"Oh, no," Jana said, turning to Melanie. "Beth's getting theatrical again. She's doing a drunk routine."

Beth picked up the empty wine bottle and held it upside down over her cup. "Oh, well," she remarked, grinning as everybody watched. "I guess I'll have to tell jokes instead. Does anybody know what you get when you cross a turtle with Dracula?"

Kids started gathering closer around Beth.

"No," replied Joel Murphy. "What do you get?"

"The world's slowest vampire!" she announced triumphantly.

The crowd roared with laughter.

"Uh-oh. They're encouraging her," said Melanie, muffling a giggle. "You'd think they'd know better by now."

Beth bowed low to the applause and pretended to stagger a little. "So what do you get when you cross an elephant with a jar of peanut butter?"

This time she didn't wait for anyone in the crowd to ask. "You get an elephant that sticks to the roof of your mouth!"

When the kids started laughing again, Jana grinned at Melanie and motioned toward the refreshments with a nod. "Let's see what's left to eat. This could go on all night."

"How could you be hungry?" asked Melanie. "I saw you eat three slices of pizza and a couple of brownies. I only had two slices of pizza and one brownie, and I'm stuffed!"

Jana grinned at her friend. "I have a tapeworm, and I need to feed it," she said matter-of-factly.

Melanie rolled her eyes and followed Jana as she threaded her way through the crowd toward the refreshments on the bar. Actually, Jana wasn't hungry, either. It was an excuse to find Randy and see what he was doing. It had been almost an hour since they had danced, and with this big crowd she had lost track of him. She was a little worried that he might be mad at her for drinking the wine, if he saw her do it. And she didn't know if he had tried it himself. She knew one thing—she wouldn't be able to relax until she found out.

I'm just being paranoid, she told herself sternly. He's probably just hanging around with some of the boys. Still, ever since they had broken up temporarily to date other people, she had been extra cautious about taking their romance for granted.

Of course the breakup had been her idea, and the whole plan was just to make sure they really cared about each other. But still, that was when he spent so much time with Sara Sawyer, who told everybody that she'd had a crush on him practically forever.

Jana frowned. She had been worrying that he might be staying away from her because he was mad at her for drinking the wine. It hadn't occurred to her until just this second that he might be with another girl.

"And come to think of it," Jana mumbled to herself, "where is Sara Sawyer right now?"

Jana grabbed a handful of pretzels and scanned the crowd at this end of the room. "You haven't seen Randy anywhere, have you?" she asked Melanie.

"Not for a whi . . . whoops!" said Melanie, her eyebrows shooting up. "Uh-oh. Don't look now. He's talking to the enemy."

The enemy? Jana whirled around. Randy was just a few feet away, deep in conversation with Laura Mc-Call. Jana's heart almost stopped. She turned back around quickly, not wanting anyone to see her staring at them and think she was jealous.

"Laura probably trapped him into talking to her," Jana whispered to Melanie. "I'm sure he'll manage to get away from her in a minute."

Melanie nodded and didn't say anything.

Jana munched on a pretzel. She was keeping her back to Randy, but Melanie was standing so she could see everything.

"What's happening?" Jana asked impatiently.

Melanie shrugged. "Same."

Jana rolled her eyes in disgust. Maybe I should stroll over there and break it up, she thought angrily, but she knew she would never do a thing like that. She shot a questioning look back at Melanie.

"Same," Melanie repeated. "She's really giving him an earful. Hold it. Laura's walking away." Her face broke into a smile. "Okay, Jana, he's all yours."

Jana nodded, taking a deep breath to calm her racing heart. Surely nothing was going on between Randy and Laura, Jana thought, not that Laura wouldn't love to break us up.

A moment later Randy walked toward her. "Hey, there you are. I was wondering what happened to you."

"I saw you," Jana replied, trying hard to keep anger out of her voice, "but I didn't want to interrupt you and Laura."

Randy sighed, and Jana knew instantly that she hadn't fooled him. He knew she was mad.

"Come on, Jana," he said. "Laura's not so bad. You and your friends ought to give her a chance. She has problems like everybody else, you know."

Jana had to bite her tongue to keep from giving him a nasty answer. "Why don't we dance once more," she said instead. "It's almost time to go home."

"Sure," agreed Randy, his easy smile returning.

He didn't mention Laura again during the rest of the party or when he took her home and kissed her goodnight, but Jana had an ominous feeling that Laura McCall was up to something, as usual.

CHAPTER

4

As Jana headed for her locker at school Monday morning, everybody was still talking about Shawnie's party. And when Shawnie herself arrived at school, Sara Sawyer, Lisa Snow, and Dekeisha Adams were waiting at her locker.

"Hey! Hey! What can we say? Shawnie Pendergast saved the day!" they shouted, imitating Beth's cheer. All four girls broke up laughing.

"That was such a *cool* party," said Lisa, and Sara and Dekeisha nodded happily.

"Well, we have something big to celebrate, don't we?" asked Shawnie. "If you think that was something, just wait until next year and see what kind of parties I give then."

24

Jana watched from across the hall. What did Shawnie mean by that? she wondered. Two bottles of wine instead of one?

"Why the funny expression?" Beth asked, coming up beside Jana.

"Oh, it's just Shawnie. She's feeling like such a big deal over the party."

"I'm not surprised. I had a blast," Beth told her. "She's probably the most popular girl in Wacko after Saturday night. And Katie said she just heard Tammy Lucero telling a bunch of kids that Shawnie should be class president next year because she's so cool."

"Well, I had fun, too, but the more I think about it, I'm not so sure serving wine was very cool," replied Jana. When Beth didn't argue, Jana glanced at her and was surprised to see a faraway look in her eyes. "What's the matter, Beth? Is something wrong?"

Beth didn't say anything for a moment. "Not really. At least I don't think so. Except . . ." Shrugging helplessly, she said, "Oh, I don't know what to think. Can you keep a secret?"

"Of course I can keep a secret," Jana said. "I'm your best friend, remember?"

Beth looked sheepish. "I know. I didn't mean it that way. It's just . . . well, it's sort of private."

"Maybe it will make you feel better to talk about it," offered Jana.

Beth nodded. "You're right. Here goes. It happened

about ten o'clock Saturday morning. For once in my life I was home alone. Dad was playing golf. Mom and Alicia had gone shopping. Todd had slept over at a friend's house. Brittany was getting her hair cut, and Brian was at work at the supermarket. I mean, it was heaven! Until the doorbell rang."

Beth paused—probably for dramatic effect, thought Jana—but at the same instant the first bell rang for classes.

"Oh, my gosh. I don't have time to finish telling you right now," gushed Beth. "I'll see you in the cafeteria at noon." She slammed her locker shut and dashed down the hall, leaving Jana shaking her head and staring after her.

"It's something private and it happened when the doorbell rang?" Jana mumbled to herself as she hurried to her own homeroom. What kind of sense did that make?

For the rest of the morning Jana had trouble concentrating. Between listening to the rave reviews most kids gave Shawnie's party and wondering about Beth's mysterious experience, it was impossible for her to keep her mind on class work.

When lunchtime finally arrived, she grabbed her lunch bag out of her locker and raced to the cafeteria. Beth was already there, sitting at The Fabulous Five's favorite table with Katie and Melanie and nibbling on a tuna sandwich.

"So, what happened when the doorbell rang?" Jana

burst out when she reached the table. "I've been going crazy all morning wondering about it." Then, realizing that Katie and Melanie might not know what she was talking about, she put her hand over her mouth and said, "Oops. Did I blow it?"

Beth shook her head. "It's okay. I was going to tell them, anyway." While Jana took out her jelly and cream cheese sandwich and began to eat, Beth told the others the part of the story that Jana had already heard.

"There was this big truck sitting in the driveway from some parcel service, and a man standing on the front porch with a huge package." Beth drew an invisible package in the air that was at least three feet high.

"Gosh, what was in it?" asked Melanie.

"Well, first off, it wasn't for me," replied Beth. "It was for my mom. She orders stuff from catalogs all the time, and I just figured it was something like that. I signed for it and started dragging it into the foyer when I noticed a rip in the side of the box. Naturally, I had to look in."

Beth paused, glancing around to see if she had everybody's complete attention.

"Don't stop now," shouted Katie, and some girls at the next table looked around to see what all the commotion was about. "What was in it?"

Beth's expression got serious, and she took a deep breath. "Disposable diapers," she said softly. "A ton of them, and they were addressed to *my mom*."

Nobody said anything for a moment.

"Do you think . . . ?" Jana ventured, but she couldn't finish the sentence. Surely the Barrys weren't going to have another baby. They had five kids already.

"I don't know what else to think," replied Beth. Her voice was barely above a whisper. "I mean, why would a big package of disposable diapers come for Mom unless . . . ?" Her voice trailed off glumly, and she looked first at one of her friends and then at another as if searching for a better explanation. "I wanted to tell you Saturday night at the party, but I just couldn't," she added.

"I don't think it would be so bad," offered Katie.

"Me, either," said Jana. "I'd love to have a baby around."

"No, you wouldn't," Beth retorted. "I can remember when Alicia was a baby, and it was not fun! Besides, since I'm the middle child, nobody pays any attention to me as it is. Boy, talk about getting lost in the crowd."

Jana tried to keep from smiling. She remembered all the times Beth had done crazy things to get her parents to notice her. Jana's favorite was the time Beth wanted to ask her parents' permission to have a slumber party, but she couldn't get a word in edgewise. That was when she used Halloween makeup to make herself look as if she'd been in an accident. She got her parents' attention, all right, but they grounded her for that one.

"How does your mom look?" asked Melanie.

"The same," said Beth. "Believe me, the first thing I did when she and Alicia got home was check her out. She's as skinny as ever."

"Well, what about Brittany?" asked Katie. "Could they be for her?"

Beth thought a moment and then shook her head. "Brittany's pretty crazy, but not *that* crazy."

"Well, what did your mother say about it when she got home and saw the box?" Jana asked.

Beth looked sheepish. "She didn't see it. I hid it in the garage under a pile of old rugs."

"You *what*?" exclaimed Katie.

"I hid it. I just wasn't ready to deal with babies and stuff right now. I wanted to think about it a little first and talk to you guys. I'll give it to her . . . later."

Just then Dekeisha Adams ran up to their table, interrupting the conversation. "Hey, guys, guess what I just heard! A bunch of kids are going to bring drinks on the class trip this weekend."

"You're kidding!" cried Jana, instantly forgetting all about Beth and her problem.

"No, I'm not," insisted Dekeisha. "See that group of kids over by the tray return? Well, that's what they're talking about."

Jana and her friends turned in unison to look. Clarence Marshall was talking a mile a minute to about a dozen kids, including Shawnie, Laura and her three best friends, Keith Masterson, and Richie Corrierro.

"You should hear what they're saying," Dekeisha went on. "Clarence and Laura say they can get all they want from home without anybody's knowing it. Richie and Keith say they can get some, too, and Shawnie is even going to try. Then, they say, they're going to sneak it on the bus in thermoses and drink it right under the teachers' noses. Doesn't that sound cool?"

"No, it doesn't," said Jana. "It sounds awful." The party Saturday night had been one thing, she thought, but taking booze on a school trip was something else altogether.

"They'll never get away with it," Katie added, lifting her nose in the air. "Do they think the teachers are stupid? They're bound to smell it."

"Oh, they're planning for that," Dekeisha assured her. "They're going to bring breath mints and chewing gum and air spray and things like that. They'll get away with it, all right. Just you wait and see. Gotta go now. Catch you later."

The Fabulous Five watched in shocked silence as Dekeisha hurried away.

CHAPTER

5

*J*ana had a terrible time falling asleep that night. Part of her couldn't believe that Clarence and Laura and the others were really going to sneak alcohol aboard the school bus Saturday when the class went into New York City to visit the Statue of Liberty and Ellis Island. But another part of her was terribly afraid that was exactly what they would do. Even Dekeisha thought it was a cool idea, and she was usually pretty sensible. What was happening to everybody? Did going into the eighth grade mean you automatically started doing things such as drinking? Surely not. But still, that was the way most kids were acting. Jana shivered. She didn't like that idea *at all*. Celebrating the end of the school year with a class trip had seemed like such a fantastic idea at first. They would leave from the school at the crack of dawn and ride into New York City in a caravan of yellow buses, yelling and singing all the way, she was sure. Then they would board the ferryboat at Battery Park, which was at the very bottom tip of Manhattan Island, for the short ride out to Ellis Island. After they toured the facilities there, they would get on another ferryboat for the short hop to the Statue, where they would get to climb up inside Miss Liberty before heading back home. It ought to be just about the most perfect day of the whole school year, but now, with so many kids talking about drinking, it could turn into a disaster.

Jana stared into the darkness. Something else was bothering her, too. Her father. She couldn't get it out of her mind that his drinking had broken up her family. And now her mother was married again, to Pink, which was short for Wallace Pinkerton. And her father had gotten married again, also, to a woman he said was going to help him quit drinking. Was this how he had gotten started? she wondered. Sneaking alcohol aboard a school bus in a thermos? She shivered at the thought. Maybe she should ask him in her next letter—*if* he ever answered her last three.

When Jana turned in her permission slip for the class trip in homeroom the next morning, Mr. Neal handed her an information sheet on the trip. She scanned it, noticing that they were to be at school to catch the bus at six A.M. sharp, and that they would be returning to the school at approximately eight P.M. But the item that jumped off the page and caught her eye was number six. *Bring a bag lunch and a drink, preferably in a thermos, since the bus has no refrigeration.*

"Boy," she said half aloud, "how could the school be so dumb? They're playing right into Clarence's and Laura's hands."

Randy had followed her into the classroom. "What are you mumbling about?" he asked. He was grinning, as usual.

"This." Jana pointed to the lunch instructions. "I suppose you've heard that a bunch of kids are planning to sneak booze onto the bus."

He nodded. "Let's face it, a few kids always like to show off, but I'll bet that most of them chicken out before Saturday."

"I sure hope you're right," said Jana.

They couldn't talk anymore because the bell rang and Mr. Neal began taking roll. Jana went to her seat, glancing across the room at Laura. She's definitely one of the ringleaders, Jana thought. Laura had been extra crabby lately, and it made Jana furious to think that she was talking other kids into doing something so stupid. Randy might be right that some kids would chicken out, but Jana had a feeling that Laura wouldn't be one of them.

She was still thinking about Laura after school when The Fabulous Five scooted into a booth at Bumpers. As usual, the fast-food restaurant was crowded with kids from Wakeman Junior High.

"All anybody can talk about is what's going to happen Saturday on the trip," said Melanie.

"Yeah. Shawnie really started something, didn't she?" replied Beth, and Jana detected an air of admiration in her voice.

"Beth, what's the matter with you?" Jana demanded. "You act as if it's okay and that Shawnie's really a big deal."

"You're off your rocker," Katie added wryly.

"Oh, come on, you guys," said Beth. "You know I don't mean it that way. It's just that sometimes you're too serious, Jana. And you, too, Katie. You need to loosen up a little." Beth held up her hand as Katie started to fire back a reply. "Let me finish. I guess that I don't really see any harm in what those kids are planning to do. Kids have always done stuff like that. I asked Brian last night, and he admitted that some guys brought beer on one of his school trips, and nobody ever found out. He said it was a hoot."

Jana couldn't believe what she was hearing. "Beth! What's wrong with you?"

Anger began creeping into Beth's voice. "Nothing. What's the matter with *you*? Nobody's going to get drunk, you know. It's just a little way of celebrating being promoted into eighth grade. And it will be fun sneaking it behind the teachers' backs. Besides, you drank some wine at the party, Jana."

"I know I did," Jana admitted.

"I saw you grinning. You thought it was fun then," Beth told her.

"I know that, too, but I also know that it was *dumb*, and now you're acting dumb! I just don't—"

Jana felt Melanie's hand on her arm. "Hey, you two. Cool it," Melanie whispered. "Here comes Alexis."

Alexis Duvall came toward them, wearing a glum face. "Hi, guys. Can I sit with you?"

"Of course," replied Melanie. "What's wrong?"

Alexis sighed. "All Lisa and Sara and Marcie can talk about is partying on the class trip. It really scares me. I don't want to, and I know you guys won't have anything to do with it, either."

Katie gave Beth a look of triumph and said, "You bet we won't. We'll all stick together Saturday, too."

Beth didn't say anything. She leaned back into a corner of the booth with a sulky look on her face. Jana couldn't swallow around the lump in her throat. Beth was her very best friend in the world, and they hadn't come this close to fighting in a long time. Was their friendship going to change because Jana thought it was wrong to drink alcohol and Beth didn't? What was the matter with Beth, anyway? Was she so worried that her mother was pregnant that she was going berserk?

A noise near the booth startled her, and she looked up to see a bunch of girls marching toward them. Shawnie Pendergast was in the lead, followed by Marcie Bee, Sara Sawyer, Lisa Snow, Laura McCall, Tammy Lucero, and Melissa McConnell. They were giggling among themselves as if they knew some terrific joke on The Fabulous Five and Alexis.

Jana cocked an eyebrow at them as they approached. "What's so funny?" she asked.

"Just you guys," said Shawnie. She exchanged glances with Laura. "You're such *babies*."

"What!" demanded Katie, almost jumping out of the booth.

"You heard me, Shannon. I said you're babies. You're afraid the big, bad teachers will catch you being naughty on the trip," Shawnie said, talking baby talk.

"And they might tell your mommies and daddies," added Laura, and the whole group broke up giggling.

They moved together toward the door and out of Bumpers before Jana and her friends could recover enough from their astonishment to speak.

"The *nerve* of those . . . those . . ." Katie fumed. She looked totally flabbergasted as she searched for words to express her anger.

"How could they say those things?" asked Melanie, shaking her head in bewilderment.

"What did I tell you?" said Alexis. "Everybody's all

caught up with partying, and now they're making fun of anyone who doesn't want to."

Jana glanced at Beth. She hadn't changed expressions through the whole episode with Shawnie and Laura. What was she thinking? Jana wondered. Is she on their side, or ours?

CHAPTER

6

That afternoon Jana didn't get a chance to talk to Beth privately at Bumpers. There was always somebody around, and Jana hadn't wanted an audience. When she started her homework after supper, she knew she could never concentrate until she got her feelings off her chest, so she went back into the kitchen and called Beth's house.

Naturally the line was busy. With five kids, and three of them teenagers, it was busy a lot. On the third try she got through.

"Hi. This is the Barrys'. Brittany speaking."

"Oh, hi, Brittany. This is Jana. May I speak to Beth?"

Brittany sighed loudly. "Okay," she said reluctantly,

"but don't talk too long. I'm expecting a very important call."

When *aren't* you expecting a very important call? Jana wondered, but she didn't say it. Brittany was always hogging the phone.

Jana heard Brittany yell for Beth, and after an eternity Beth picked up the receiver.

Jana felt almost shy. "Hi, Beth. I'm sorry we almost had a fight today."

"Me, too," said Beth.

"Are you still mad at me because I don't want to drink?"

"I don't want to drink, either!" Beth answered in an exasperated tone. "I can't believe you really think I do. It's just that you guys are making such a big deal over nothing."

"It's not nothing, Beth," Jana insisted.

Beth groaned loudly. "Forget it then, okay? I don't think we should discuss it right now."

"You're probably right," replied Jana, deciding that compromise was the best thing for the moment. Beth was obviously still pretty worked up, and Jana didn't want their argument to get any bigger.

"And guess what else happened to me today," offered Beth.

Jana braced for what might be coming next. "What?"

"After supper I was still a little hungry, so I was

rummaging around in the pantry, when I found baby food."

"Baby food?" Jana repeated in astonishment.

"Six jars. You know what that means, don't you? First a ton of disposable diapers, and now six jars of baby food."

Jana's heart ached for Beth. This was obviously not good news. "Did you talk to your mom about it?" she asked. "Maybe they're left over from Alicia."

"I don't think so. They weren't even dusty. Besides, I dig around in there all the time. I would have seen them if they'd been in there very long."

"Yeah, I guess you would," agreed Jana. "So I guess you haven't asked her about the diapers, either, huh?"

"No," said Beth. "I just don't want to deal with it yet. I mean, can you imagine this house with *six* kids in it?"

"Not really," Jana conceded.

"And do you realize that I'll get stuck baby-sitting all the time," Beth complained, almost blasting out Jana's ear, "and I probably won't even get paid!"

Jana couldn't help laughing, and when they hung up a few minutes later, she felt better. Beth may have been acting strange earlier, but she was back to her old dramatic self now.

*   *   *

Jana was almost to school the next morning when she saw Funny Hawthorne standing on the next corner, apparently waiting for someone. Funny was the fourth member of Laura McCall's clique, The Fantastic Foursome, but ever since they began working together on the yearbook staff, Jana had decided Funny was different from the other three. She wasn't nasty or obnoxious like Laura, Tammy, and Melissa. She was sincere and kind, and just as her name suggested, she had a terrific sense of humor.

When Funny spotted Jana, she began waving, and Jana hurried to join her.

"I'm glad I caught you before we got to school," Funny said as Jana stopped beside her to catch her breath.

"Me, too," said Jana. "What's up?"

Funny frowned as the two sauntered toward school. "I heard what happened at Bumpers yesterday. Tammy called me last night and bragged about it."

"It was no big deal," Jana told her. "It doesn't really matter what they think, or even what they say. We can handle it."

"Hey, I know that." Funny flashed a big smile at Jana. "It's just that Shawnie and Laura are talking more and more girls into being on their side, and Tammy said the only thing they're worried about is that one of you might tip off the teachers before the trip."

Jana stopped in her tracks. "Tip off the teachers! You

know we would never do a thing like that. We're not snitches!"

"Of course *I* know that," Funny assured her, "and they will, too, if they'll just think about it. But you know how Laura is. I thought it might be a good idea to warn you."

"Thanks," murmured Jana. The idea was so incredible that all she could do was shake her head in wonder.

"There's one other thing," Funny added, hesitation in her voice. "I don't know if I can get away with it or not, but I'd really rather be with you guys—especially on Saturday. I'm really not into partying, if you know what I mean."

Jana smiled sympathetically. She still couldn't understand why Funny hung around with the other three, but she did understand how tough it could be to side with someone else instead of your friends.

"Of course you can be with us. Alexis wants to, also. It'll be fun, and we'll just ignore those other kids."

"Thanks, Jana," Funny said softly. "I knew you'd understand."

Jana and Funny went their separate ways when they reached the school ground, and Jana found the rest of The Fabulous Five already at their favorite spot by the fence. She smiled to herself as she got close enough to hear Melanie talking about her favorite subject: boys.

"I'm dying to know how many boys are going to

bring stuff on the bus," she said. "Probably a lot of them. You know what show-offs most boys are."

"Well, I know Randy isn't," chimed in Jana.

"Tony had better not, if he knows what's good for him," said Katie.

"You don't really think he would, do you?" asked Jana.

"Not really." Katie grinned. "He *acts* a lot more macho than he really is."

"I keep wondering about Shane," said Melanie. "I mean, his parents used to be hippies. He may not see anything wrong with it. I'd die if he got in trouble."

"I don't think he'll get involved," replied Jana. "He's too laid back. He doesn't need to prove anything to anybody."

"Yeah," said Melanie, brightening. "You're probably right. At least, I hope so."

"On the other hand," added Katie, "guys really like to impress each other and brag about what they've done. And they hate to be teased. Some of them may do it just to keep from being teased."

"True," agreed Melanie. "But I sure hope you're wrong this time."

Jana noticed that Beth hadn't joined in the conversation. Oh, well, she thought, that's her problem.

She couldn't help feeling confident about Randy as they headed for their lockers. He didn't need to impress the other guys. They all respected him and looked up to him. And he'd never worry about being teased. There was no way anyone could talk him into drinking on the trip.

She glanced around as she entered the building and then stopped in her tracks. There was Randy, leaning against the trophy case beside the office, and he was talking to Laura McCall.

CHAPTER

7

*J*ana stood there, blinking back tears of jealousy and rage. How dare Laura try to sink her claws into Randy and work on him to join her party crowd? That was obviously what she was doing.

Laura glanced up. Seeing Jana, she let a smile twitch around her mouth for an instant, and then she looked at Randy and went on talking.

Jana whirled around and stomped down the hall, aware that she was going in the opposite direction of her locker, but not caring.

Maybe I should rat on Laura and the others, after all, she thought angrily as she turned down a hall that ran through the center of the building and would take her to her locker without having to pass Laura and Randy again. Maybe I should write a note and sneak it into Mr. Bell's mailbox by the office door. Or maybe I could call the school and disguise my voice.

Jana sighed. She couldn't do either of those things, and she knew it. It was not just that she would never snitch, no matter what. There was Randy. What if Laura really had persuaded him to go along with her crowd? Then if Jana ratted, he would get in trouble, too. She could never be responsible for a thing like that.

When she reached her locker, she worked the combination lock, remembering suddenly that she had forgotten all about telling her friends the warning she had received from Funny. She would have to tell them at lunch, because there was no way of knowing what Laura might be cooking up.

As she swung open her locker door, she heard a crash, followed by the sound of glass breaking near her feet. Before she could look down, the strong smell of liquor rose toward her and made her cough.

"Oh, my gosh!" Jana cried. "Where did *that* come from?"

Scattered at her feet were fragments of a bottle, a few of them lying in small, brownish puddles. Some of the liquid had splashed onto her white tennis shoes and the legs of her jeans.

"Pe-YEW!" said Mona Vaughn, who was standing at her locker next to Jana's. Mona made a face and pretended to gag.

"Yeah. Where *did* that come from?" asked Heather Clark.

Jana was too flustered to answer for a moment. "I don't know . . . honest . . ." she faltered. "I don't have *any* idea!"

By now a large crowd had gathered.

"Hey, Jana's starting the party early," yelled Tony Sanchez, and laughter rang in the hall.

"Somebody get Mr. Bartosik," called out Joel Murphy.

Jana panicked at the mention of the custodian's name. "No! Don't call him. I can clean it up myself."

"It's too late," said Mona. "Somebody already went to get him."

"Oh, no," Jana murmured.

"What's going on?" asked Katie, elbowing her way through the crowd.

Jana almost collapsed with relief at the sight of her friend. "Somebody planted a booze bottle in my locker, and it fell out and broke when I opened the door. Thank goodness it was almost empty."

Melanie and Beth walked up in time to hear Jana's explanation.

"Who do you think did it?" asked Beth.

"I *know* who did it," said Jana, and then she told them what Funny had said on the way to school.

Katie frowned. "How could Laura or anyone else get into your locker? Didn't you lock it when you went home last night?"

Jana was stunned. "Of course I locked it last night. I just unlocked it right now. But you're right. Nobody knows the combination to my lock. Not even the rest of The Fabulous Five."

"Then you're going to have a hard time explaining this," Katie told her.

"Explaining it!" Jana exploded. "Why should I have to explain it? You know I didn't put that bottle in there myself!"

"Calm down, Jana," said Katie. "I know you didn't put it there, but Mr. Bartosik will have to report it to Mr. Bell, and then you'll probably have to go before Teen Court. I just want you to be prepared for the questions the judges will ask."

Jana groaned. "Not Teen Court. What will I say?"

Just then Mr. Bartosik came through the crowd, pushing a cart that contained a trash barrel, a broom, a mop, and a bucket of water.

"Been an accident here, huh?" he said pleasantly, but his expression changed as he sniffed the air. "Young lady, is that what I think it is?"

Jana gulped. "I . . . I think so, but I didn't put it in there," she insisted. "I just opened my locker, and the bottle fell out. I don't know where it came from."

The custodian gave her a look that said, "A likely story," and went to work cleaning up the mess.

It was almost time for the bell, and kids drifted back

to their own lockers to put away their jackets and get out their books for classes.

Jana turned to Katie again. "What am I going to do?"

"I don't know, unless you can find out who put that bottle in there *and* how they got into your locker. Otherwise, Teen Court won't have much choice but to find you guilty of bringing booze to school."

"Oh, Jana, this is awful." Melanie put her arms around Jana and gave her a big hug. "I wish there were something we could do."

Jana couldn't stop the anguish welling up inside her. "Booze! Liquor! Alcohol! Why was it ever invented? All it ever does is cause trouble! *Especially in my life!*" she said, thinking of her father. She stomped off down the hall, leaving her friends to stare after her.

Sinking into her seat in homeroom a few minutes later, Jana let her mind travel back to when she was three and a half. She wasn't sure if she really remembered what happened then or if she had heard about it so often that it seemed real.

She was sitting on the back steps with her father just as the sun was coming up. He had awakened her and carried her out into the fresh morning air to tell her good-bye.

"I'm going to get myself straightened up," he had said, speaking just above a whisper. "I'm going to stop drinking so that your mother will let me come home again. In the meantime, you be a good girl and do what your mother says."

Then he had kissed her on the forehead and led her back to bed. That was the last time she had ever seen him, because he hadn't stopped drinking. He had gotten worse. And because of that, he never came to see her and hardly ever wrote her letters, even at Christmas.

But a few months ago things had changed. He had written her a long letter about a woman he had met. Her name was Erma Benfield, and she was helping him stop drinking. In fact, at the end of the letter he had said they were getting married. Since then, Jana and her father had exchanged several letters, and each of the ones he wrote sounded more happy and optimistic than the one before. He definitely had stopped drinking, and he had gotten a job since he and Erma had married.

And then, without warning, the letters had stopped. Jana had been puzzled for a while, but eventually she understood.

"It's that Erma Benfield—or Erma Morgan, now," she had told Beth. "She isn't letting Dad see my letters."

"Why would she do a thing like that?" Beth had asked.

"Because she's jealous. She's probably afraid that my dad and I will get close again and then she'll lose him.

I'm sure that's what's happening. It's the only thing that makes sense."

"You don't think the reason could be that your dad started drinking again?" Beth had asked. "That happens to people sometimes, you know."

Jana had frowned. "That, too," she said. "For all I know Erma may be encouraging him to drink again. She may be nervous about his writing to me and be trying to put a stop to it by getting him drunk. I certainly wouldn't put it past her."

"That wasn't exactly what I meant," Beth had said, but Jana hadn't heard. She was too busy conjuring up pictures in her mind of her father and Erma, sharing a bottle of liquor while her letters lay buried in the wastebasket.

The bell ending homeroom shook Jana out of her daydream. She hadn't heard a single thing that went on during the period.

She was heading for the door when Mr. Neal called to her.

"Jana, I just got a note that you're supposed to report to the office right away. Mr. Bell would like to see you."

She swallowed hard and tried to keep her expression blank, but inside she was quaking.

"Okay," she murmured, and hurried into the hall.

CHAPTER

8

Jana had never seen Mr. Bell looking so stern.

"Sit down, Jana. We have something very serious to discuss."

She perched on the edge of the chair beside his desk, balling her hands into tight fists to keep them from shaking.

"I suppose you know why I've sent for you this morning," the principal went on.

Jana nodded and looked at the floor. She wanted desperately to explain that she had not put the bottle into her locker, that it was a dirty, rotten trick played on her by someone who wanted to get her in trouble, but she knew she would never be able to force the words out around the lump in her throat. In fact, the lump was growing bigger every second.

"Mr. Bartosik told me about the accident at your locker, and I saw the pieces of bottle, as well as smelled them," he said. "Now, I'd like for you to tell me what happened. Take your time. Just explain it to me in your own words."

"I . . . I can't, sir," she began timidly. "I mean, I can't explain *how* it happened. All I know is that I opened my locker, and the bottle fell out. I didn't put it there. I swear I didn't."

"Am I to understand that you forgot to lock your locker last night and someone simply opened the door and put the bottle inside after you were gone?"

Jana blinked at him in surprise. It was too good to be true. Mr. Bell was actually giving her an easy way out of this awful mess. "I guess so," she said quickly before she could lose her nerve.

"Well, you've certainly been an exemplary student, so I would find it hard to believe that you placed the bottle there yourself," he said.

Relief surged through Jana. He really did believe her.

"Do you have any idea who could be angry enough at you to do such a spiteful thing?" asked Mr. Bell. He leaned across the desk and added, "I'd like very much to find out who the culprit is."

"No," Jana lied. "Maybe . . ."

"Maybe what?" Mr. Bell prompted.

"Well, maybe someone was just looking for some-place to hide it and accidentally found my locker," she offered.

Mr. Bell gave her a skeptical look. "Maybe," he said solemnly, "but if you think of anyone who might have done it on purpose, please let me know. You may go back to class now."

Jana nodded. She murmured, "Thank you," and got out of the office as fast as she could.

By lunchtime her insides had stopped shaking, and around bites of her jelly and cream cheese sandwich, she told Beth and Katie and Melanie about her trip to the principal's office.

Katie looked at her in astonishment. "Jana Morgan, do you mean you actually *lied* to Mr. Bell?"

"What else could I do?" demanded Jana. "I could have admitted my locker was locked, and then he would have believed I put the bottle in there myself. Or I could have said Laura did it, but that wouldn't have explained how she got into my locker, and he would *still* have believed I did it and that I was trying to pin the blame on someone else."

"I agree with you, Jana," said Beth. "You would have been dead if you'd told the truth."

"Well, at least it's over, and you didn't get into trouble," said Melanie.

"Wait a minute," added Beth. "Maybe it isn't over. If

Laura could get into your locker once, she could do it again."

Jana's heart sank. "You're right. I didn't think of that." Then she brightened again. "I know. I'll change my lock."

"The trouble is," Beth went on, "you don't know what kind of system she's got. Even if you change locks, there's no guarantee that she won't be able to get in again."

"Gee, Beth, you're full of cheerful news," complained Katie. "I think if Jana changes her lock, she'll be okay, especially if she gets a lock with a key instead of a combination. Laura may have been smart enough to figure out Jana's combination once, but she'd have to be a genius to get into a lock with a key."

"And we all know she's no genius," Jana commented wryly. "I think I'll get a new lock after school. Anybody want to head for the mall with me?"

"I can't," replied Melanie.

"Me, either," said Katie.

Jana looked at Beth.

Beth sighed. "Actually I could, but if you don't mind, I'd rather go on home and check the pantry for more baby food."

"You still haven't talked to your mom?" asked Melanie.

Beth shook her head. "I know I should, and I've started to a couple of times, but I always chicken out.

And she's been acting funny, too. Take last night. I walked into the den, and Mom and Dad suddenly stopped talking and gave me one of those big, fake grins. I know something's up, and I *know* what it *is*. Why don't they just come out and tell us?"

"You've got to remember that they don't know you know," said Melanie. "I think they're just waiting for a special moment. They may even be planning a party or something."

Beth made a face. "Listen to the romantic," she said, nodding toward Melanie. Then she grinned. "I think they're just afraid the five of us will gang up on them and refuse to baby-sit with the little brat when it gets here."

"Or charge ten bucks an hour," suggested Katie.

"Hey, now that's what I call a super idea," said Beth, and they all laughed.

Jana was rounding a corner between fifth and sixth periods when she saw Funny Hawthorne walking ahead of her, and an idea occurred to her.

"Hey, Funny, wait up," she called.

Funny flashed a big grin as Jana caught up with her. "What's up?"

"You mean you haven't heard?" Jana asked in astonishment. Then she filled Funny in on the disaster at her locker and her interview with Mr. Bell.

"Wow," replied Funny, "Laura really works fast. I

knew she was thinking of doing something to you. I told you about that this morning. But I had no idea she had already done it."

"Well, she did," said Jana. She took a deep breath. "And I need to ask you a big favor."

"What is it?" asked Funny.

"Do you think you could find out how she did it? I mean, my locker was locked, and somehow she managed to get it open so she could plant that bottle. I'm going to change my lock, but I'm still worried. If she could do it once, what's to stop her from doing it again?"

Funny whistled low. "I see what you mean. Gosh, Jana, I have no idea how she did it. I'm really the odd man out in a lot of her schemes, especially anything to do with you. Laura knows you and I are friends, and she hates it. But maybe I can find out something. I'll try. I promise."

"Thanks. You're a terrific friend." Looking at Funny's sunny smile, she said, "You know, Funny, sometimes I just can't . . ." She broke off, shaking her head.

"Sometimes you just can't what?" asked Funny. "Understand why I stay friends with Laura?"

Jana nodded sheepishly.

"Don't forget, Laura and I've been friends for a long time. We started kindergarten together." Funny looked as though she were going to add something, then seemed to change her mind. "I don't know. I guess I just don't feel as if I can desert her right now." She giggled and added, "But I'll have to admit that she was a lot nicer in kindergarten."

After they parted to go to their separate classes, Jana was still thinking about Funny. Laura doesn't realize what a loyal friend she has, Jana mused, but I just hope that loyalty won't keep Funny from helping me now.

CHAPTER

9

Teachers were still able to keep some discipline in the classrooms on Thursday, but by Friday, Wacko Junior High was a zoo. Kids were running and pushing in the halls and talking and passing notes in the classrooms, right under the teachers' noses. The cafeteria wasn't any better, but fortunately, thought Jana, no one started a food fight.

"I can't believe that tomorrow is our class trip and that next Wednesday school will be out for the summer and we won't be seventh-graders anymore," said Melanie when The Fabulous Five were strolling on the school ground after lunch.

"I don't know why they don't just dismiss us today and get it over with," commented Beth.

Jana smiled. She knew what was coming next.

"You know perfectly well that the school has to get in a certain number of class days to get money from the government," Katie said, "and we had so many snow days during the winter that they had to extend the school year into next week."

"Of course I know that," replied Beth, rolling her eyes. "It's just that everybody is so hyped up that holding classes next week will only be a waste of time."

Just then Jana had the feeling that someone was looking at her. Turning around, she saw Funny leaning against a tree, first glancing her way and then peeking around the other side of the tree back toward the building. Maybe she's found out how Laura managed to get into my locker, thought Jana.

"I'll be back in a minute," she said. "I need to talk to Funny."

Hurrying to her, Jana asked, "What's up? You look as if you're hiding from someone."

"I am," Funny told her. "I don't want Laura or the others to see me talking to you right now, because I just found out how Laura got into your locker."

Jana's pulse quickened. "You did? How?"

Funny breathed a deep sigh. "You're not going to believe this, but Laura is so paranoid about her friends that sometimes she insists one of us do something to prove our loyalty."

"Yes, I believe it," Jana assured her. "There have been rumors about it ever since school started."

"Well—" Funny hesitated. "You're going to *hate* this, but here goes. Sometime around Christmas Laura was mad at Melissa for something, and she told Melissa that the only way she could prove her friendship to Laura was to stand close enough to spy on you when you were opening your locker and get the combination to your lock."

"You're kidding!" Jana's mouth dropped open, and she looked around helplessly. "And Melissa actually did a thing like that? She got the combination to my lock?"

When Funny didn't answer, Jana shook her head and said, "Silly question, huh? Obviously she did, and Laura has been waiting all this time for the perfect moment to use it." Jana stared at the ground, anger welling up inside her.

"Right," said Funny. "She was so afraid you'd tell on her and the other kids who plan to drink that she thought she'd scare you off by getting you in trouble first."

"Well, it didn't work," said Jana.

"I've got to run," Funny said anxiously. "Laura and Tammy and Melissa stopped in the girls' rest room, but they should be out by now and heading this way."

Jana nodded. "Thanks, Funny. I appreciate what you've done for me."

"I'm really sorry about all this," Funny murmured, and Jana knew she was sincere.

Funny started to leave, but Jana called out, "Wait a minute. One more quick question. How did you find out?"

"I overheard Laura and Melissa talking about it a few minutes ago. Laura was bragging about how easy it had been to pull that on you, but Melissa is really scared someone will find out and she'll get in trouble."

I'll bet she is, thought Jana as Funny hurried away. Melissa's whole life involves being perfect. Straight A's; officer in two or three clubs; perfection with a capital P. Getting in trouble would totally humiliate her. But she deserves it, Jana thought angrily. She shouldn't get away with a thing like that, and neither should Laura!

Jana stomped back over to her friends and repeated what she had just heard from Funny. "Can you believe that Laura would do a thing like that?" she demanded.

"*Yes*," chorused the others.

"I think you should get revenge," remarked Beth.

"Me, too," agreed Melanie.

"If you could prove it, you could take her to Teen Court," offered Katie.

"No, I couldn't. Today after school is the last session of Teen Court for this school year," Jana reminded her. "You're on the Court—how could you forget a thing like that?"

"Whoops." Katie grinned sheepishly.

"Maybe you could do something on the trip tomorrow," said Beth. She rubbed her hands together and grinned slyly. "Like rat on her."

Jana shook her head. "I couldn't, not even on Laura. But that's not the only reason. I'd get a lot of other kids in trouble, too, like Dekeisha, and Sara, and Lisa. And *you!*" she added emphatically.

Beth looked embarrassed, but she didn't say anything.

"I'm sure we can think of something else," said Melanie. "Something that will just get Laura and Melissa."

"Sure," Jana said without conviction. Getting revenge would only lead to more trouble between The Fantastic Foursome and The Fabulous Five, and she had had enough of that for one year.

Later that evening Jana was fixing her lunch for the trip and thinking about her predicament with Laura when the phone rang. It was Randy.

"I thought you'd be at Bumpers tonight, since the rest of The Fab Five were there," he told her. "Everybody's pretty excited about tomorrow, and the place was a madhouse."

"I'm glad you missed me," Jana replied with a catch in her throat. "But I had a lot of things to do tonight." And a lot of things to think about, she added silently. "Besides, I want to be wide awake when the bus leaves at six o'clock in the morning."

"Yeah. Me, too. It's going to be tough," said Randy. "Hey, by the way, what's this I hear about a liquor bottle falling out of your locker this morning? It isn't true, is it?"

It was all Jana could do to keep from telling him the truth about how Laura had gotten the combination to her locker and planted the bottle inside to get her in trouble, but she didn't. Since she couldn't actually prove it was Laura who did it, it would sound like gossip, and Randy hated gossip.

"I'm afraid it is true," she answered. "I must have left my locker unlocked last night and somebody played a nasty joke."

"That's awful," said Randy. "Do you know who did it?"

"I have an idea, but I can't prove anything." Jana hesitated. "Randy," she went on slowly, "there's something I'd really like to ask you."

"Sure. Is something wrong?" he asked.

"Not exactly, but . . . well, maybe," Jana fumbled.

"Maybe you'd better tell me what it is." Jana could hear concern in his voice.

Jana sighed. "It's just that it seems every time I look around lately, you're talking to Laura McCall. You know we don't get along very well, and I guess it just bothers me, that's all."

"It shouldn't. You know you're the only one I like."

When Jana didn't answer, Randy added, "Is that all that's bothering you, or is there more?"

Jana bit her lower lip. She couldn't fool him, so she'd better get the rest of it off her chest. "No, I keep wondering if you're going to be partying with Laura and Shawnie and all the other kids tomorrow."

"Hey, you know I wouldn't do that," Randy said. "Just because some of those kids are my friends doesn't mean I'll go along with everything they do. I thought you knew me better than that."

"I do," Jana insisted. "It's just that Laura's been hanging around you so much this past week, and I know she's planning to drink on the bus. I kept wondering if she was trying to get you to join in."

"Aw, come on. Don't be silly," said Randy. He was trying to sound as if he was teasing, but Jana could tell that he was serious.

What do you mean, don't be silly? she wanted to shout. Still, a memory was beginning to nag at her. She had gotten jealous of Randy's attention to Laura once before. She had even run out of Bumpers and straight into the path of a car because she was angry at him. Randy had been a hero. He had pushed her aside and been hit by the car himself and was in a coma for days and days. It was only later that she had found out the truth. Laura had a crush on Shane, and she had been asking Randy to put in a good word for her. Jana bit her lip. She had been wrong about Laura that time. Maybe she was wrong this time, too.

"Hey, are you still there?" asked Randy.

"Yes," she said in a small voice.

"I'm sorry if things looked funny," he said. "Honest. It's just that Laura has needed some friendly advice lately, and for some reason she asked me."

"What kind of advice?" Jana asked stiffly, her old suspicions coming back again.

"Sorry," said Randy. "She asked me not to talk about it to anyone."

"Oh," Jana mumbled. A few minutes later they said good-night and hung up. Jana headed upstairs to get ready for bed. She looked at herself in the mirror while she brushed her teeth, wondering why she didn't feel better. Randy had said he wasn't going to drink tomorrow and that Laura was only asking for friendly advice. That should be good news.

But instead of feeling better, what she really felt was angry and confused.

CHAPTER

10

*I*t was still pitch-black when Jana's stepfather dropped her off in front of Wakeman Junior High the next morning, but the lights at Wakeman were blazing. In front of the building kids milled around, waiting to board the string of buses at the curb.

"Jana! Jana! Over here!"

Katie was waving from the front steps, and Jana could see that she was the last of The Fabulous Five to arrive. Melanie was yawning and gazing off in the distance as if she were still half asleep. Beth was sitting on the steps, wearing earphones and rocking back and forth to music coming from the small tape player attached to her belt. Jana felt a flutter of excitement as she rushed to join them. This was going to be fun.

Alexis Duvall reached Katie, Beth, and Melanie at the same time Jana did. "Bummer," she grumbled. "The bus assignments are according to homeroom, which means that since we're split into different homerooms, we won't all be able to sit together."

"Oh, no," complained Beth. "They can't split us up! It won't be any fun if we can't sit together."

"We'll be together on the boat and at Ellis Island and the Statue of Liberty," said Katie. "That's most of the time."

"Yeah, but it's on the bus when some of the kids are going to bring out their thermoses," Alexis reminded them.

Jana didn't say anything. On one hand, she was glad that Randy would be on her bus, since none of the other Fab Five members were. But on the other hand, Laura McCall, Tammy Lucero, and Clarence Marshall were on her bus, too.

"The first bus must be yours, Jana," said Beth. "Mr. Neal's waiting there."

Jana nodded and glanced toward the line of buses.

"Wow!" Melanie shouted. "Look who one of your chaperons is. Mr. Arrington. Shane's dad. Oh, Jana. You're so lucky. I'd give anything to trade places with you."

A tall, thin man in jeans and a T-shirt was leaning against the first bus in line. His blond hair was trimmed into a rattail at the back of his neck, and he was deep in conversation with Jana's homeroom teacher. Jana blinked in surprise at the sight of Mr. Neal, who looked more handsome than ever in an open-necked sport shirt and trim-fitting jeans. It seemed strange to see a teacher in casual clothes. She remembered with a twinge of nostalgia how she had had a huge crush on Mr. Neal when he was her teacher in fifth grade.

"And that must be your other chaperon," commented Katie. "Can that possibly be Curtis Trowbridge's mother?"

"No way," said Beth as they all stared at the attractive dark-haired woman with Curtis who was approaching Mr. Neal and Mr. Arrington. She was wearing high-heeled sandals, a bright-colored sundress, and fashionable sunglasses.

"How can a nerdy kid like Curtis have such a great-looking mom?" asked Melanie.

Jana laughed. "Maybe he takes after his dad."

Just then Mr. Bell went past them and up to the top of the school steps, calling for everyone's attention.

When most kids had quieted down, he said in a loud voice, "Good morning, everybody! Are you ready to start your trip?"

The applause was so wild that Jana looked around the quiet residential neighborhood and wondered if anyone in the surrounding houses could possibly still be asleep.

The principal shushed the crowd again.

"Your homeroom teacher will be standing beside the bus you are assigned to ride. It's time to board now. Have a wonderful day!"

A few kids applauded, but most made mad dashes toward the buses.

"I'll see you guys at the boat dock in Battery Park," Jana called out to the rest of The Fabulous Five.

As she joined the crowd pushing to board her bus, she looked around, hoping to spot Randy, but she didn't see him.

"Take your time, everybody," cautioned Mr. Neal. "There are plenty of seats, and the bus won't leave until everyone is on board."

As soon as Jana climbed on, she saw Randy. He had a pair of seats midway down the aisle, and he was motioning to her. It wasn't until she reached him and slid into the seat beside the window that she realized they were sitting directly behind Laura McCall and Tammy Lucero. Jana frowned. Had Randy done that on purpose?

Mr. Neal took roll and introduced the chaperons, then made an announcement. "Okay, everybody, listen up. These old school buses travel pretty slowly, so it's going to take us awhile to get into the city. In the meantime, I want everybody to stay seated. No jumping around. You can talk and sing songs, but keep the noise level to a roar. The chaperons and I are going to be in the front of the bus, so let us know if you have any problems."

"Like if somebody gets carsick and pukes?" Clarence yelled from the back of the bus, and then guffawed at his own joke.

Mr. Neal frowned but didn't respond.

"When can we eat our lunches?" asked Heather Clark.

"We'll have lunch at the Statue of Liberty," replied the teacher. "There are outdoor picnic tables, and we should get there just before noon."

"I'll starve by then," muttered someone toward the front.

"It's okay if we take a drink out of our thermoses, though, isn't it?" asked Laura. She grinned at Tammy and winked.

Mr. Neal nodded. "But just be careful. We don't need any messes to clean up."

A bunch of kids giggled at that, and Jana leaned toward Randy and said, "This is making me nervous. Do you think those kids will really do it?"

Randy shrugged. "I hope not, but Clarence and some of the others think they're pretty big deals. I wouldn't put it past them."

Jana looked around the bus. Almost all the seats were taken. Shane Arrington and Tony Sanchez were directly behind her and Randy. Clarence and Joel Murphy were horsing around in the very last seat in the back.

By the time the buses pulled onto the turnpike a few minutes later, the air was filled with excited chatter.

Outside, the sun was turning the sky a gorgeous shade of pink.

Randy closed Jana's hand in his and gave her a reassuring smile. "I bet we'll have a blast today, no matter what the other kids do."

Just then someone began singing the Wakeman fight song, and everyone joined in.

"Hey, this is the last time we'll be able to sing 'Go! Fight! Win! Wakeman Junior High!'" said Curtis when the singing died down. "From now on it will be Wakeman Middle School."

"Right!" yelled Derek Travelstead. "Let's sing it again!"

"Same song, second verse, a little bit louder, and a little bit worse," chanted Laura and Tammy.

The kids sang it a second time and then a third. That was followed by chorus after chorus of "On Top of Spaghetti."

By about the twelfth chorus, Jana started to relax. Nobody really had the nerve to bring booze on this bus, much less drink it, she decided.

She whispered her feeling to Randy, adding, "Why would anyone want to spoil such a good time by doing something like that, anyway?"

Before Randy could respond, Jana saw Tammy turn to Melissa McConnell, who was sitting across the aisle from her. "It's time to bring out the thermoses," Tammy whispered. "Pass it on."

CHAPTER

11

*J*ana cringed at Tammy's words. "Did you hear that?" she whispered to Randy.

Randy nodded, and Jana could see by his expression that he felt as miserable about it as she did. Together they watched as the word spread through the bus like wildfire. Some girls put hands over their mouths and giggled. A few others gasped.

"What are we going to do?" Jana asked Randy.

He shrugged. "There's nothing we can do but stay out of it."

Jana nodded and slumped back in her seat. She knew Randy was right, but that didn't help much.

Out of the corner of her eye she saw Derek Travelstead inch out of his seat in the back and waddle up the aisle. When he reached Tony and Shane, he held his thermos out toward them. "Hey, man. Have some!"

Tammy whirled around in her seat and shot Derek a fierce look. "*Shhhhh!*" Then she put her hand over her mouth to muffle the sound of her words and growled, "Get back to your seat before the chaperons see you and figure out what's going on."

Derek crouched lower and whispered hoarsely, "I was just gonna share this with my old buddies, Tony and Shane."

"You heard what she said," muttered Shane. "Get out of here and stop being stupid."

"Hey, what's the matter, Arrington?" Derek said, his voice getting louder. "I never thought you'd wimp out."

"It's probably because his old man's a chaperon," said Joel Murphy, who had left his seat in the back and come forward, too.

Shane scowled, but he didn't say anything.

Randy saw Jana looking at Shane with concern. "Don't worry about Shane. He won't let anyone get to him."

Jana nodded and nervously bit her lower lip, peering through the kids in front of her toward the front rows of the bus, where the chaperons sat. *Come on*, she pleaded silently. *Somebody turn around and stop this before it goes any farther*. But Mr. Neal, Mr. Arrington, and Mrs.

Trowbridge were all staring out the windows at the scenery.

"Have you seen anybody drink anything yet?" Jana asked Randy a few minutes later.

"No," he replied.

"I haven't, either," she whispered. But she kept her eyes firmly fixed on Laura, and a few minutes later saw Laura slowly unscrew the top to her thermos.

Jana poked Randy in the side, then nodded toward Laura. "Can't you give her a little more *friendly advice?*" she grumbled.

"It wouldn't do any good," said Randy.

Suddenly from the back of the bus Clarence Marshall burst into song. "Ninety-nine bottles of beer on the

wall . . . ninety-nine bottles of beer . . ."

Kids all over the bus started laughing, and several joined in.

"If one of those bottles happened to fall . . . ninety-eight bottles of beer on the wall!"

"Isn't this a riot?" said Tammy, bouncing up and down in her seat.

"Right." Laura laughed. "How dumb can Mr. Neal and the chaperons get?"

Jana had heard all she could take. She had been staring at the back of Laura's head and seething with anger over Laura's putting the empty bottle in her locker to make it look as if Jana were drinking. Fortunately, Laura's little trick hadn't worked, and Jana had forced herself not to have it out with Laura over that because it would only get Funny in trouble. But this was too much. Leaning forward, she tapped Laura on the shoulder. "Laura McCall, you'd better stop all this right now, before you get everyone on the bus in a lot of trouble."

"Oh," cooed Laura, "is the little baby . . ." She stopped abruptly as Randy leaned forward also, fixing her with an icy glare. "Hey, I couldn't stop it even if I wanted to," she added, trying suddenly to look innocent. "Everybody's doing their own thing."

Jana looked around. She would have to admit that now that the kids had actually started sneaking drinks, the chaperons were probably the only ones who could stop it. And they didn't even know what was going on!

Although she didn't actually see anyone drinking, she did see chewing gum and breath mints being passed around, and every so often she would hear the soft hiss of a spray can, which she knew was room deodorizer. Still, she felt certain she could smell the faint, sickly sweet odor of alcohol in the air. Or is it my imagination? she wondered.

Sighing, she settled back and stared out the window, wondering what was happening on the other buses. Were the kids sipping out of their thermoses, too? Maybe not, she thought, since Laura and Clarence were the real ringleaders, and they were both on her bus. But she couldn't forget about Shawnie and some of the others who thought sneaking around under the teachers' and chaperons' noses was going to be a blast. They were probably just as much into it as the kids on this bus, Jana thought.

Then Jana remembered Beth and swallowed hard. When it came right down to it, would Beth back off, or would she go along with the crowd? Jana wished she could be sure that Beth would be smart, but nobody loved to clown around and party more than Beth. If Beth didn't take the whole thing seriously, she just might do the wrong thing.

Before long Jana noticed that the song was down to fifty-seven bottles of beer on the wall, and the bus had entered the outskirts of New York City, which meant the buildings were drab and squeezed together, and the traffic was bumper to bumper.

When the bus stopped at a traffic light, Mr. Neal got up and walked slowly down the aisle and back again. Kids snapped to attention, and thermos bottles disappeared from sight as all eyes were riveted on the teacher.

Jana held her breath. Did he know? Could he smell it, too?

But her hopes faded when he reached the front of the bus again, raised his hand for the singing to stop, and said, "We'll be there in a little while, so I want you all to look around your seats to make sure you have all your belongings—especially your lunches—because the buses won't be coming on board the ferry with us."

Laughter rippled through the bus.

"I also want you to remember your bus number. This is bus number one . . . seven . . . two . . . six. Seventeen-twenty-six. Memorize it. Write it on your arm. Do whatever you have to, but don't forget it. There will be school buses from a lot of schools at the park when we get back, and we don't want anyone getting lost and boarding the wrong bus."

By the time Mr. Neal had finished his instructions about walking in an orderly manner from the buses to the dock, good conduct on the boat and at Ellis Island and the Statue of Liberty, and all the other rules and regulations pertaining to the day, they were pulling into the parking lot at Battery Park.

"Hey, I see the Statue!" Curtis shouted, and pointed to the middle of New York Harbor.

"Well, we got this far without any trouble," Jana said to Randy as the bus pulled to a stop.

She hadn't been talking to Laura, but Laura must have overheard her, because she turned around and looked at Jana with an air of superiority.

"Of course," Laura remarked airily. "What did you expect? Don't forget, we're the big deals on campus now."

CHAPTER

12

*K*ids pushed and shoved their way into the aisles,
and Jana felt herself being swept along toward the exit.
Once she was out of the bus, she clutched her lunch
bag and looked around for the rest of The Fabulous
Five. Randy had stopped to talk to Shane, but he had
promised to meet her again on the boat.

"Jana! Jana! You should have been on our bus!"
Melanie came running up to Jana, her face glowing.
"Scott Daly and Keith Masterson almost got caught."

"You're kidding," said Jana. "What happened?"

By this time Katie and Beth had joined them, and
Melanie pulled all three closer and said, "Keith had a
thermos of stuff, and he offered some to Scott. Scott
was acting like a big deal and bragging about how

drinking it was nothing. Then he took a big swallow and almost choked! He was gagging and spitting, and tears were squirting into his eyes. It was a riot."

"Oh, my gosh," said Beth. "Then what happened?"

"Well, Miss Dickinson rushed back to see what was happening. You could tell she was scared. She probably thought he was having a heart attack or something. But when he saw her coming, he grabbed his own thermos and acted as if he had just swallowed wrong and choked."

"But couldn't Miss Dickinson smell anything?" asked Jana.

"Ha! Talk about quick thinking," replied Melanie. "Sara Sawyer started squirting perfume all over the place and brushing her hair and pretending that she was trying to look good before she got off the bus."

"Do you mean to say that Miss Dickinson got that close and still didn't catch on?" Jana asked in disbelief.

"Exactly," said Melanie. "Whew! Talk about a close call."

"Hey, everybody," said Beth. "Let's forget about all that stuff and have fun, okay?"

"I'll go along with that," agreed Katie. "Let's find Alexis. She wants to hang around with us today."

"So does Funny," added Jana. She was glad they xere changing the subject. And she was especially glad that Beth had suggested it. Maybe she had worried about Beth for nothing, she thought with relief. And if the other kids wanted to act up, let them, she thought. Nothing's going to spoil our day.

They found Alexis and Funny, and all six girls locked arms and walked toward the dock in a line.

"How'd you get away from Laura and the others?" asked Jana as they walked along.

"I just told her that I didn't want to be in on the partying and neither did Alexis so we were going to hang out together for today," said Funny. Then she giggled and added, "She'll probably freak out when she sees that Alexis and I are with you guys. Don't worry, though. I'll think of some big excuse."

"Hey, everybody, let's pretend we're a Broadway chorus line," said Beth. She stopped and stuck out her right foot. "Everybody start on your right foot."

Giggling, the others put their right feet in front, too.

"Now, when I say GO, step out on your right, and we'll do one—two—three—KICK!" called out Beth. "Ready? Here goes. *GO!* One—two—three—KICK. One—two—three—KICK."

Jana had trouble juggling her lunch and thermos of juice and hanging onto Beth's and Melanie's arms at the same time, but she managed, and it was fun. Pretty soon other girls were running over to join the line, hooking arms and kicking. Dekeisha Adams and Lisa Snow grabbed onto one end, and Marcie Bee and Heather Clark got on the other. A second line formed behind them, and even a few boys got into the act and started clowning around.

"Hey, look at me! I'm a ballerina!" cried Clarence Marshall in a falsetto voice. He was hopping on one foot and twirling around, waving to the crowd and blowing kisses.

Jana threw back her head and laughed. So these are the kids who are going to be the big deals of Wakeman Middle School next year, she thought. That's pretty funny.

As they got closer to the dock, they saw the huge ferryboat pulling into its berth to discharge a load of passengers.

"Look! There's our boat!" cried Mona Vaughn. "It's three decks high."

"I'm getting on the top deck!" shouted Joel Murphy.

"Me, too," said Richie Corrierro and several others.

"Wait a minute, everybody!" shouted Mr. Neal over the noise of the crowd. "Line up over here for your tickets, and remember how you're supposed to behave."

The homeroom teachers passed out the boat tickets, which were the only tickets they would need during the entire trip, and a brochure on both Ellis Island and the Statue of Liberty. By this time the ferry had unloaded its passengers and was ready to take aboard new ones.

"Hurry," Beth urged as The Fabulous Five, Alexis, and Funny made their way toward the gangplank together. "I've seen three other schools here already. We don't want them to get all the good seats."

They raced aboard on the lower deck and hurried up the stairs to the second deck.

"Want to stop here?" asked Melanie. "There's a snack bar on this deck."

"No, come on," urged Beth. "We want to be on the top deck, where we can see everything. You can always come back down if you want something from the snack bar."

Melanie made a face, but she followed Beth up the last flight of steps and out onto the open deck. It was already getting crowded, and the girls were lucky to find a place to squeeze in next to the railing.

"There they are," said Jana, pointing out first toward the enormous statue of the lady holding a torch and then to a small island that was mostly covered by a large brick building with a red roof.

"Oh, neat," exclaimed Katie. "Just think, this is exactly what all those millions of immigrants saw when they began coming to America a hundred years ago. Doesn't it make you feel special?"

Jana felt a tingle of excitement at Katie's words. It did make her feel special. She closed her eyes and tried to imagine what it must have been like to stand on the bow of an immigrant ship, instead of the Circle Line ferry, carrying everything she owned in the world and praying that she would be allowed to stay in this great country.

Even Melanie seemed impressed as she squinted into the sunshine. "Wow. I bet it was really scary," she murmured.

The ride out to Ellis Island took only a few minutes. The boat pulled up to the dock and let out its gangplank, and hundreds of passengers poured ashore.

Jana had looked for Randy on the boat, but she hadn't seen him. Now, on shore, the crowd seemed larger than ever.

"How am I ever going to find him?" she mumbled to herself.

The girls wandered through the front doors of the main building and into a vast, high-ceilinged room marked "Baggage Room" on their maps. Jana steered Katie in the right direction, since she was busy reading out loud from the brochure.

"'Basking in the shadow of the Statue of Liberty, the newly established Ellis Island Immigrant Station answered the lady's plea to "Give me your tired, your poor, / Your huddled masses yearning to breathe free," when it officially opened its doors to the world on Friday, January 1, 1892,'" read Katie. "Isn't that a beautiful poem?"

"Yeah," said Jana, "but you'd better watch where you're going."

"Hey, guys, there's a gift shop," Melanie cried, pointing down a hallway to the right of the front door. "Let's go there first."

"I'm broke," said Alexis.

"Me, too," said Jana, "besides, I want to see this place. It's really pretty interesting."

"Yeah," agreed Funny. "Let's look at some of the displays. We can always go to the gift shop later."

Katie, who had continued reading her brochure while the others discussed the gift shop, suddenly stopped, her face radiant with excitement. "Everybody! Listen to this. 'Perhaps it was fitting that a fifteen-year-old Irish girl named Annie Moore was the first to be questioned in the immigrant station's second-floor Registry Room, because America, like young Annie, was in its adolescence.'"

Melanie made a face. "So?"

"*So?* What do you mean, so?" Katie demanded. "Didn't you hear me? It says right here that the first immigrant to come through Ellis Island was a woman!"

"Oh, Katie," groaned Jana, "you're too much."

The girls wandered through the baggage room on the first floor, looking at examples of the funny, old-fashioned luggage the immigrants had brought. They watched a movie and then went upstairs, following the route the new Americans had followed as they were given medical exams and then told if they could remain in America or had to go back home.

Finally, after the girls made a quick trip into the gift

shop to please Melanie, it was time to board the ferry again and head for the Statue of Liberty.

"Isn't it awful that some of the immigrants had to go back home just because they got sick on the ships on their way to America?" asked Funny as they walked toward the ferry.

Jana nodded, but she didn't say anything. She had been keeping an eye out for Randy as they'd toured the displays, but she hadn't seen him. Now, as they boarded the boat, she thought she caught a glimpse of him sitting in a chair on the second deck. He had his back to the railing and was talking to someone, but she couldn't see who it was.

The crowd was moving at a snail's pace as it wound through the bottom deck and toward the stairway leading to the upper decks. Jana tried to press through the crowd, but all she got was angry looks from the passengers ahead of her.

Finally she made her way up the steps and onto the second deck. It was Randy. Her heart fluttered, and then almost stopped beating completely.

Randy was there, all right, and he was engaged in earnest conversation with Laura McCall.

CHAPTER

13

*J*ana hurried on past Randy and Laura, pretending she didn't see them and making her way up to the top deck. Her heart was bursting. This was supposed to be a special day, and Randy was spending all his time with Laura McCall. She kept her face turned toward the water so that her friends couldn't see the tears in her eyes, and if they noticed anything, they didn't let on.

"I think I'll die if we don't get to eat pretty soon," lamented Melanie.

"Me, too," said Beth. "I'm starved."

"Miss Dickinson said that there are picnic tables by the Statue and we can have our lunch there," said Alexis.

"Terrific," said the others.

Jana had completely lost her appetite, and it didn't return when a few minutes later, they found a table in the shadow of the giant statue and began spreading out their lunches. When they had come back down from the top deck to get off the ferry, she had looked again for Randy and Laura. Neither was there, and now Laura was with Melissa and Tammy at a nearby table, and Jana had seen Randy talking to Scott Daly.

Jana had been gazing absently in Laura's direction, silently brooding about all the time Laura had spent with Randy, but now Jana focused on Laura's face. Something was wrong, but Jana wasn't sure what it was.

Tammy and Melissa seemed to be pleading with Laura about something, but Laura wasn't having any part of it. Shaking her head angrily, she cast her half-eaten sandwich aside and began taking big gulps from her thermos.

Uh-oh, thought Jana. Laura's really going after that stuff.

Jana turned to Funny, who was sitting beside her and watching Laura, too.

"Did you see what I saw?" Jana whispered.

Funny nodded. "I'm not surprised, though. Laura's been acting strange lately. I think she's got trouble at home."

"Laura?" Jana asked in astonishment. A little more sarcastically, she added, "I thought Laura had the most perfect home life on earth."

"Yeah, that's what she wants everyone to think," said Funny.

Jana started to make a nasty remark, but she remembered the incident a few months ago when Laura had tried to convince everyone that she had a maid. Maybe things weren't as great for Laura as she tried to pretend.

"So what kind of problem is she having?" asked Jana.

Funny looked at Jana apprehensively, then sighed. "Promise you won't tell anyone, but I think something's wrong between Laura and her dad."

"Humpf," sniffed Jana. "I thought her dad worshipped her and let her get away with murder."

"That's what everybody thought, including the rest of The Fantastic Foursome," Funny said. "But ever since he got a big promotion a few weeks ago, Laura's been talking about how he spends a lot of evenings and weekends at the office, leaving her home alone. And when he is home, his girlfriend, Trudy, is always there. If you want my opinion, I think it's making Laura miserable."

"But what does that have to do with drinking?" asked Jana.

"Who knows?" said Funny. "I really shouldn't be talking about her problems to anyone—except I know I can trust you not to tell anyone—but she really has me worried."

No one else heard their conversation. Melanie was gazing around, probably looking for Shane, and Beth and Alexis were talking together. As usual, Katie was munching on a carrot stick and reading the brochure on Ellis Island and the Statue.

"Oh, my gosh. This is too good to be true!" she cried, and Jana looked away from Laura to see what Katie was excited about now.

"Don't keep us in suspense," said Alexis. "What's so great?"

"Listen to this," replied Katie. "You know that poem I like so much? The one that starts, 'Give me your tired, your poor, / Your huddled masses yearning to breathe free, / The wretched refuse of your teeming shore—'"

"Yes! Yes! We know the poem," Beth said impatiently. "So, what about it?"

Katie gave her a disgusted look. "Well, it just so happens that it was written by Emma Lazarus—*another woman*." Katie made a sweeping gesture, taking in both the Statue of Liberty and Ellis Island. "Do you realize that without *women* this whole place might not exist!"

"Wow," said Melanie in a reverent voice. She looked at both Ellis Island and the Statue and said, "That's really special."

Funny's tinkling laughter rang out. "Oh, Katie. I can't believe you sometimes."

"Well, let me tell you, women just don't realize the important role they've played in history," Katie huffed.

Beth had been flipping through her brochure. Now

she stopped and pointed toward a page. "Unfortunately, here's one thing a woman didn't do. It says here that the Statue of Liberty was designed and built by a man. His name was Frédéric-Auguste Bartholdi. I guess we just can't win 'em all, can we?"

Everybody laughed, including Katie.

"I'm ready to climb the stairs inside the Statue," Funny announced. "I'm going all the way up to the crown and look out."

"Me, too," said Melanie. "Yipes!" she cried, doing a double take as she looked in her brochure. "It says here that there are three hundred sixty-five steps that we have to climb."

"Right," chimed in Katie. "It's the same height as a twenty-two-story building. There are some other interesting facts in the brochure, too. Did you know that the Statue's nose is four feet six inches long?"

Funny burst out giggling. "What a nose! Wouldn't you hate to be up there when she sneezes?"

"Yeah," said Beth. Her eyes grew big as she visualized the scene. "You'd end up on Manhattan Island, hanging on the pointy top of the Empire State Building!"

The girls gathered up their lunch mess, tossed it into a trash can, and headed for the base of the Statue, still reading statistics from the brochure.

"Her hand is sixteen feet five inches in length," offered Alexis.

"And her fingernails are thirteen inches long by ten inches wide," continued Melanie, holding out a hand and examining her own nails. "Can you imagine how much polish it would take to do all ten?"

When they went inside the base of the Statue, they stopped briefly to look at some of the displays and then headed for the stairs. There was a line leading to the staircase, but it moved quickly, and soon they were on their way up.

Jana felt a rush of excitement as she started the climb. The clang of footsteps on the metal staircase and the voices of the climbers echoed above her. Behind her marched Funny and Alexis and the rest of The Fabulous Five.

The farther up they climbed, the quieter everyone got, and soon they were puffing and panting with every step.

"I'm glad I didn't eat too much lunch," remarked Jana when they stopped once about halfway up to get their breath.

"Me, too," agreed Alexis. "My stomach feels a little funny as it is."

"Your stomach feels a little *me*?" Funny teased, and they all started up again.

They had climbed only a little farther when Jana heard familiar voices ahead of them.

"Laura, what's the matter?"

"Are you okay? Do you need to sit down?"

The voices belonged to Tammy and Melissa, and Jana turned around to Funny and frowned.

"What do you think is going on?" Jana asked.

Funny shrugged. "I don't know, but it sounds as if Laura has a problem. Maybe she slipped or something."

"Maybe," murmured Jana.

As they continued the climb, Jana listened for more sounds from Laura or Melissa or Tammy. Something must be wrong with Laura for the other two to shout so loudly, she thought.

Suddenly she heard Tammy again.

"Oh, Laura! No!"

Then there was a loud retching sound, and the smell of vomit filled the air.

"Pe-YEW! Somebody barfed!" shouted a boy in front of Jana.

"Yuck! Puke! It's running down the stairs!" yelled someone else.

Jana and her friends stood plastered against the wall in horror as slimy, yellowish vomit trickled down the stairs beside them.

Nobody on the staircase moved or said anything for a couple of minutes. Then there was the sound of footsteps coming down from above. When Jana saw that it was Melissa and Tammy helping Laura back down, she turned her face away. She couldn't look at them, even though she felt a surprising rush of sympathy for

Laura. It must be the most embarrassing moment of her life, Jana thought.

After the three girls had gotten past, the rest of the crowd resumed the climb, holding their noses as they stepped carefully around the mess on the stairs. And when Jana stepped into the crown and looked out one of the openings, the sight was so beautiful that she temporarily forgot all about Laura McCall.

"Look," she said to the others, "there's the Verrazano Bridge, connecting Staten Island and Brooklyn. Beyond it is the Atlantic Ocean. That's the way all the immigrants' boats came in."

"Yeah, the boats from England definitely came that way," murmured Melanie.

She and Jana stared silently at each other for a moment.

"Are you thinking what I'm thinking?" Jana asked.

Melanie nodded, and they said in unison, "Christie."

"I really miss her," said Melanie.

"Me, too," Jana told her. "I wish she was with us right now."

"Don't forget, she's coming home this summer," said Katie, who was standing beside Melanie. "And one of the first things she'll see when her plane gets to America is the Statue of Liberty!"

"Yea!" they all shouted.

"Hey, maybe she'll have to stop at Ellis Island," teased Beth, "and she'll be dressed like an immigrant and carry all her stuff in a big wicker basket. I can see it all now. Her tennis racquet will be poking out the top of the basket."

Jana shook her head and grinned. "There you go again, Beth, getting totally carried away."

Because of the size of the crowd, they had to move quickly through the crown and down again.

"It went fast, but it was still fun," said Katie as they sat down on the grass outside the Statue to rest.

"Yeah, I loved it, too," added Beth. "Even if Laura almost spoiled it by throwing up."

The girls nodded and exchanged glances, and then Katie nudged Jana. "Uh-oh," she said, looking sharply to the left. "Randy's motioning to me to get your attention."

Jana whirled around. Randy was standing beside one of the picnic tables. He was alone, and he smiled when she looked at him.

"Hi, Jana. Can I talk to you?"

She stared silently at him for a moment. Part of her was really mad at him for spending so much time with Laura. Another part of her was hurt and disappointed that they hadn't spent the day with each other the way they had planned. But the biggest part of her still cared about him too much not to listen to his side of the story, so she excused herself from the others and went to him.

CHAPTER

14

"You're mad, aren't you?" Randy asked in a quiet voice.

Jana sighed and answered him as honestly as she could. "I don't want to be, but I guess I am . . . a little bit."

Randy nodded that he understood. "I guess I don't blame you. I know we planned to be together today."

"Yeah," Jana said wistfully, "it was supposed to be a pretty special day."

Randy shifted from one foot to the other. "And I wrecked it by spending so much time with Laura."

All Jana could do was nod.

"I'm not sure I understand everything that's going on myself," Randy began. "Laura's been acting pretty obnoxious in some of our classes lately. I guess she could tell I didn't like it because she's also been hanging around a lot as if she wants to talk about something. Maybe explain. Or apologize. I don't know, but when I try to pin her down and find out what's bothering her, she clams up."

"But didn't you tell me yesterday that you've tried to give her a little friendly advice?" Jana reminded him.

Randy looked sheepish. "Yeah, she was yelling at Funny in front of everyone in the hall a couple of days ago, and I told her I thought she ought to cool it. Naturally she didn't listen."

"I know she thinks you're an especially nice person. Everybody does. And I also know this isn't the first time she's come to you for help. But what I can't figure out is why is she making such a big deal over drinking?" Jana insisted.

Randy sighed. "I don't know for sure, but from little things she's said about her life at home, my guess is that she and her dad are having problems. She acts pretty miserable and I think that she's trying to get attention. Actually I think she's desperate to get everybody to notice her."

Jana was thoughtful for a moment. "So what you're saying is, she thinks drinking is cool and that looking cool will make her more popular."

"That's pretty much the way I figure it," said Randy. "And I guess she thinks that if she's popular, maybe the stuff at home won't hurt as much."

"How can she think that?" Jana asked in astonishment.

"Look at what happened at Shawnie's party," said Randy. "The more some kids made idiots of themselves, the more other kids cheered them on."

Jana sighed, but she didn't say anything for a moment. Then she told Randy what Funny had said about Laura and her father. "In a way, I know how Laura feels," she admitted. "It's really awful when you love someone and they won't pay any attention to you. I've been trying ever since I was three years old to get my father to pay attention to me."

"At least you were too smart to try to handle your problem the way Laura did," said Randy, ruffling Jana's hair.

"Yeah," said Jana, "and you know what else? I almost feel sorry for her."

"Me, too," said Randy, "but I just don't know what else to say to her."

Jana shook her head. She didn't know, either.

Just then she heard someone calling her name. Dekeisha was running toward them, and she looked upset.

"Jana! Randy! Did you hear about Laura?" Dekeisha stopped beside them and grabbed her side, bending over to catch her breath.

"Sure," said Jana. "She threw up in the Statue."

"That's not all," Dekeisha gasped between puffs and pants. "She got sick again in the ladies' room in the base of the Statue. Miss Dickinson was in there, and now she *knows*."

"What?" exclaimed Jana.

"That's right," said Dekeisha. "And the teachers and chaperons have called a big meeting of everybody from Wacko over by the picnic tables. Come on. We'd better get over there."

Jana glanced toward the picnic area. Kids were streaming there from every direction. She exchanged worried glances with Randy, then fell in step with Dekeisha as she headed that way, too.

"Can I have everybody's attention, please?" Mr. Neal called out over the noise of the crowd when most of the Wakeman seventh-graders had assembled by the picnic area. Just about everyone quieted down, but a few boys near the back weren't paying any attention. "Listen up, back there, okay?" he yelled. This time everyone stopped talking.

Jana's heart was beating a mile a minute, and she squeezed Randy's hand. He looked down at her and smiled reassuringly.

"Something disturbing has happened today," began Mr. Neal. He gestured to include the adults standing beside him, two other teachers, Mr. Naset and Mrs. Clark, and the assorted parents who were along as chaperons. Some nodded, a few frowned, and all of them looked very serious.

"It has come to our attention that some of you brought alcoholic beverages along with you and were drinking on the bus."

There was a buzz of astonishment in the crowd as everyone tried to look shocked and innocent. Jana noticed Shawnie, who was standing near the grown-ups, shrugging and pretending to be totally amazed. A few kids farther back smirked, and some giggled.

Looking around, Jana spotted Melissa and Tammy over to one side, but she couldn't find Laura anywhere. Was Laura still sick in the ladies' room, Jana wondered, or was she just too embarrassed to come out? Just then Jana realized that Miss Dickinson wasn't with the parents and chaperons, either. She must still be with Laura, Jana thought uneasily.

"This is something we will deal with more fully at school on Monday," Mr. Neal was saying, "but for now, I'd like all the girls to go with Mrs. Clark and all of the boys to go with Mr. Naset and me. We're going into the rest rooms, and when we get there, I'd like you to form a line and each one of you to go to the sink and empty anything that's left in your thermos—no matter what."

Murmurs raced through the group, and Mr. Neal held up his hand for quiet again.

"We're not going to ask any questions, but we want

to make certain that every single thermos is empty before we get on the buses to go home. Any questions?"

From the tone of his voice, Jana knew no one would have the courage to ask any.

"See you," called Randy as the boys and girls separated to form lines and moved silently toward the base of the Statue, where the rest rooms were located. Jana noticed that now no one was looking up at the magnificent lady with her crown and torch, the way everyone had been earlier. And probably no one was thinking about her job as the welcoming committee for the immigrants coming to America, either. Or that this trip was supposed to be one of the best days of the school year.

The line of girls passed Laura and Miss Dickinson coming out of the ladies' room as they went in. Laura's eyes were red, and her face was blotchy and streaked. Jana was amazed at how terrible Laura looked, but she didn't say anything. She didn't even look at her friends. She had too many thoughts racing around in her mind.

Sure, Laura has problems, Jana thought, ones that must seem too big to solve by herself. She could even identify with some of Laura's feelings. She certainly knew how helpless it felt to have a father who ignored her most of her life, as if he didn't care about her or her feelings. And now even her stepmother was ignoring her.

Jana tried to change the subject in her head, but she couldn't. Memories were crowding in thick and fast. Like the time she had written her father a terribly nasty letter just to see if he would answer, which he didn't, and the time she had faked being sick and written him that she was on her deathbed. He hadn't answered that time, either. Those were silly things to do, but she was glad that she never tried anything as stupid as drinking alcohol to get his attention. But Laura had, Jana thought sadly, and because Laura had acted so dumb today, she had not only made a fool of herself, she had ruined the whole class trip.

One by one the girls filed past the sinks under the watchful eyes of Mrs. Clark and the women chaperons. Then they headed silently to the ferry that would take them back to their buses and home.

CHAPTER

15

*T*he trip back home was pretty quiet. Laura slumped against the window of the bus and didn't look at anyone. After a while, Jana leaned her head on Randy's shoulder and went to sleep.

But at school Monday morning no one could stop talking about what had happened on the school trip.

"And I mean to tell you, she was absolutely blotto," said Dekeisha, describing what had happened when Laura got sick again in the rest room. "She could hardly stand up."

The Fabulous Five and some of their friends were clustered at the fence before school.

Jana looked around, frowning. "Has anyone seen Laura this morning?"

"Are you kidding?" asked Katie. "I'll bet she couldn't show her face."

"I'll bet she couldn't, either," said Beth. Jana was surprised to see that Beth was looking at her as if she had something else to say.

Jana looked back at Beth, trying to say with her eyes that she would listen.

"I just want you to know," Beth began in a shaky voice, "that I did not drink anything on the bus after all. I decided you guys were right. In fact, I'm sure more kids *said* they drank on the bus than actually did."

Jana rushed forward and gave Beth a big hug. "I'm so glad you didn't," she whispered, and the others murmured their agreement.

"What do you think Mr. Bell will do?" asked Melanie. "Mr. Neal said they would deal with it today."

"The entire seventh grade will have to appear before Teen Court," piped up Beth. When no one laughed, she shrugged and said, "Who knows?"

"Well, one thing's certain," said Melanie, "school's out day after tomorrow, so he can't punish us by cancelling any more trips or anything like that."

"Are you forgetting the seventh-grade dinner dance this Saturday night?" Katie reminded them.

"Wow," said Jana. "I did forget about that, but surely he won't punish the whole class for something only a few kids did."

"I hope you're right," said Katie, "but we'll have to wait and see."

It didn't take long to find out. The bell had no sooner rung and the students gone to their homerooms when the public address system crackled to life.

"This is Mr. Bell. I would like all seventh-graders to go to the auditorium immediately for an emergency assembly."

Jana swallowed hard as the PA system went silent again. This was it. What if the whole class got in trouble for what just a few kids had done? It wouldn't be fair. She glanced across the room at Randy. He looked worried, too.

Anything could happen she told herself. She thought about the seventh-grade dinner dance again. It was a Wakeman tradition, and she and her classmates had been looking forward to it all year. Or what if Mr. Bell did something even worse. Could the kids who drank get held back in seventh grade?

Jana was amazed at how subdued the students were as they filed into the auditorium and found seats. Usually kids were horsing around and making lots of noise. But not today. They walked in in an orderly fashion and sank into seats, talking barely above a whisper.

She and Randy managed to save seats for Katie, Melanie, and Beth in the middle section near the back. There was still no sign of Laura, although Jana could see Tammy and Melanie coming down the aisle, and she had waved to Funny earlier in the hall.

Mr. Bell was sitting on the stage with the four teachers who had been on the class trip. Behind them was a blackboard on wheels.

Jana fidgeted nervously in her seat. This is silly, she scolded herself. Why should I be nervous? I didn't do anything.

When everyone was finally seated, Mr. Bell walked up to the podium and adjusted the microphone. "Good morning, boys and girls," he began cheerfully.

Nobody answered.

"I'm sure you know why I called this assembly, so let's get right down to business. It has been reported that while most of you behaved yourselves very well and had a great time on the class trip last Saturday, a few of you chose to break the law."

There was a stirring in the audience,

"That's right," Mr. Bell went on. "Alcohol consumption by minors is against the law. It is also extremely dangerous."

He paused for a moment, and Jana suspected that it was to let his remarks sink in.

"Now I'm going to ask you to help me make a couple of lists." He nodded to Mr. Neal and Mr. Naset, who rolled the blackboard forward. "The first one is all the reasons you can think of *for* drinking alcohol." He wrote "FOR" at the top of the board on the lefthand side and then drew a line down the center. "Next, let's think of all the reasons *against* drinking, especially by students your age." This time he wrote "AGAINST" on the right side of the board. "Who can give me a reason for drinking?"

The auditorium was as silent as a tomb. Kids looked around wide-eyed, waiting to see if anyone would have the courage to speak.

Mr. Bell cleared his throat, and a few kids shuffled their feet, but no one said anything.

"Can't anyone give me a reason for drinking?" urged Mr. Bell.

Just then, to Jana's amazement, Randy got slowly to his feet. "I think sometimes kids drink to forget about their problems," he said, and then sat down again.

Jana beamed at him.

"Thank you, Randy," said Mr. Bell. He turned and wrote "To forget problems" under "FOR." "Does anyone have any other ideas?"

This time there was whispering in the audience, as if a lot of kids had ideas but were afraid to speak up.

Jana looked down the row at her friends and was surprised to see Beth leaning forward in her seat. The next instant Beth jumped up.

"I have another one, Mr. Bell," she announced in a loud, clear voice. She flicked a quick glance at Jana before she went on. "A lot of kids do it because other kids pressure them and tell them it's cool."

Beth looked at Jana again as soon as she sat down. Her eyes were shining, and Jana gave her a big smile.

When no one could think of any other reasons for drinking, Mr. Bell moved over to the column labeled "AGAINST."

This time five kids stood up. Mr. Bell called on Shane first.

"It can embarrass you and make you look stupid," said Shane.

"And it's against the law," offered Whitney Larkin.

Standing next to Whitney, Curtis added, "It's addictive."

"That's what I was going to say," said Alexis, and then she sat down.

The only one left standing was Dekeisha. "It can make you *sick*," she said, making a terrible face.

When Mr. Bell had written all the reasons against drinking on the board, he turned back to the audience and said, "I am going to deal with those of you whom we know were drinking on an individual basis. Contrary to the rumor floating around, the seventh-grade dinner dance will not be cancelled."

A cheer went up, and Jana and Randy nodded and smiled at one another.

"But," Mr. Bell went on in a serious voice, "I hope all of you will make a copy of these reasons for and against drinking alcohol and take them home with you. And then I hope you'll remember them the next time someone pressures you to drink. I also hope you'll remember them when you come back to school next fall, because you're going to be the *eighth-graders*."

A small cheer went up, and Jana and Randy nodded and grinned at each other.

Mr. Bell smiled, too, and went on, "That means you're going to be the role models for all the younger students. They're going to look up to you and copy what you do. You're going to have a big responsibility, but I know you can do it. I hope when school is out Wednesday, you'll all have a wonderful summer and look forward to coming back to Wakeman Middle School in the fall."

Jana walked home later that day thinking about the school year that was ending. It had been scary at first, leaving Mark Twain Elementary for junior high. In elementary school everyone had known each other and felt secure, but junior high had changed all that, they had had to start all over, meeting new friends, testing old relationships, and establishing new places for themselves.

"But it was fun," she said aloud. "And next year's going to be fun, too." Still, she couldn't help wondering how different it would be when they were the oldest— the big deals on campus, as Clarence had said. Will The Fabulous Five stay as close as they are now? she wondered, especially now that Christie was coming back. Would they still stand in their special spot by the fence? And would their class be able to be a good influence on the younger kids? And what about Laura McCall? Would she change over the summer or come back the same?

Jana was still thinking about these things when she reached her apartment building. When she stepped inside the foyer, Mrs. Grogan, the mail carrier, was stuffing letters into the boxes.

She looked up and smiled at Jana. "Hi there. You're in luck today. I have a letter for you."

Jana looked at Mrs. Grogan in surprise. She hardly ever got mail. "Thanks," she said, and took her own letter plus the stack of bills and catalogs addressed to her mom and Pink.

There was no return address, but Jana held her breath as she looked at the postmark. *Poughkeepsie, New York*. She swallowed hard. It was from her father.

Her mother and Pink weren't home from work yet, and Jana dropped the rest of the mail on the kitchen counter and hurried to her room. Sitting down on the edge of her bed, she examined the envelope. It was definitely her father's handwriting.

Had he found all of her letters that Erma had hidden from him? Had he written to her in secret so that Erma wouldn't find out?

Jana carefully opened the envelope and took out the letter. She held her breath, almost afraid to read it.

> *Dear Jana,*
>   *I know it's been a long time since I've written, and I'm sorry about that. Erma wanted me to write sooner, but I honestly didn't know how to tell you our big news.*
>   *Jana, honey, Erma and I are expecting a baby in the fall. Isn't that wonderful? Sometimes I have to pinch myself to believe it. I can't imagine what it's going to be like with a house filled with baby bottles and diapers again. I hope I'm up to the responsibility; I'm sure going to try. It's as if my life is starting all over again. As if I'm getting a second chance now that I've sobered up.*
>   *Erma says you'll have to come and see us after the baby is born, and I want that, too.*
>   *I love you,*
>   *Dad*

Jana stared at the letter until misty tears made the words impossible to read. Her father did still care about her, and Erma hadn't been hiding her letters from him, after all. She had been wrong to blame her stepmother.

But a baby! Jana sank back against her pillow, trying

to comprehend what that was going to mean. For an instant she was angry. How dare he have a new baby to love and take care of after ignoring her all her life! It was obvious that this new person would come between her and her father now that they might be starting to get acquainted again.

Jana shook her head resolutely. "No!" she said out loud. "I won't let it be a problem. Besides, it's going to be wonderful having a sister or brother, and it's even better that Dad's getting a second chance."

Jana took a deep breath and thought of Beth. It was a shame that Beth felt so worried about the prospect of a new baby in her family. Babies, in Jana's opinion, were wonderful. Then she sat up and grinned. She ran to the phone and dialed Beth's number.

"Have I ever got something to tell you!" she practically shouted into the phone when Beth answered.

"What?" demanded Beth.

"I can't tell you over the phone," said Jana. "Can I come over right now?"

"Of course," replied Beth. Then she added, "Just a minute."

"Mom, Jana's coming over. Can she stay for supper?" Jana heard Beth call out.

Jana didn't hear Mrs. Barry's response.

"Pleeeease," Beth begged.

"Well, I guess so," said Mrs. Barry.

"Jana? Mom says terrific," Beth told her, and Jana chuckled.

A little while later the two girls were in Beth's room.

"So, what's the big secret?" asked Beth.

Jana looked at her friend and felt a smile stretch her mouth all over her face. "You're not going to believe this," she began.

"Believe what?" demanded Beth.

Taking a deep breath, Jana said, "You're not the only one who's going to have a new baby in the family."

"What!" gasped Beth. "Your mom and Pink?"

"No," said Jana. "I got a letter from my dad today. He and Erma are going to have one. Isn't that great?"

Beth looked at Jana with concern. "So that's why you haven't heard from your dad in a while. I'm glad he's not drinking again or anything like that, but are you sure you're happy about it? I mean, that little kid is going to have the dad you never had. Aren't you jealous?"

"No," Jana said quietly. "I'm glad my dad's getting a second chance. Besides, I've got Mom and Pink, and Erma's already said I have to come and see the baby as soon as it's born. That means you and I will be able to compare baby pictures."

"Yeah, but you're still luckier than I am. You live too far away to baby-sit!"

The girls were still giggling to themselves at the dinner table later on. It seemed as if Beth was feeling better about the possibility of her own family's new baby now. In fact, she had said just before they came downstairs that she thought she could handle the whole idea now.

They had barely filled their plates when Beth gave Jana a goofy smile and said, "Mom, there's something I need to tell you."

"What's that, dear?" asked Mrs. Barry.

"Well . . . a few days ago a package came for you, and I forgot to tell you about it."

"A package?" echoed Mrs. Barry, jumping to her feet. "Who is it from?"

Beth shrugged. "I don't know. I didn't pay any attention."

"Beth, you jerk," said Brittany. "Don't just sit there. Give it to her."

Beth threw her sister a disgusted look and said, "It's in the garage. It was . . . um . . . kind of big."

"Maybe it's the package you've been waiting for, honey." Mr. Barry reached over and gave his wife's hand a squeeze.

Mrs. Barry looked confused. "Well, I really was hoping for a letter instead of a package."

"Come on. Let's go see what's in it," said Brian.

The whole family and Jana followed Beth into the garage.

"It's over here under those old rugs," Beth explained sheepishly. She went to the far corner and pulled the box out from under the rugs and into the center of the room. "Here."

Mrs. Barry rushed forward and looked at the address label on the top of the box. "Oh, no," she said. "It *is* what I've been waiting for."

Beth and Jana exchanged glances. "It's a carton of disposable baby diapers," said Beth. "There's a hole in the box, and I looked in."

Suddenly Mr. and Mrs. Barry began laughing. "Oh, no!" said Mrs. Barry between laughs. "And you thought—Oh, Beth. You thought I was going to have a baby!"

"Well, of course," Beth replied indignantly. "What else was I supposed to think?"

Mrs. Barry put an arm around Beth's shoulder. "And that's why you hid them, isn't it?"

Beth nodded.

Beth's mother led her to the box. "Look at the return address on the shipping label," she instructed.

"National Sweepstakes Clearinghouse?" Beth said in a voice filled with amazement.

Mrs. Barry nodded. "I saw this sweepstakes entry blank in the grocery store," she began. "With the UPC code and labels from six jars of baby food, I could enter and try for the grand prize of a four-year college scholarship. Heaven knows we could use it with five kids in the family. So I entered. Then about three weeks ago I got a letter from the sweepstakes clearinghouse saying I was a prize winner. The only trouble is, they didn't say which prize I had won, and there were a couple of hundred smaller prizes—like a *year's supply of disposable diapers*. I've been watching the mail every day to find out what I won."

Everybody had a good laugh. Even Brittany gave Beth a sympathetic smile.

"That's wonderful," exclaimed Beth, acting absolutely giddy. "I mean—wow!" Suddenly she looked at Jana sheepishly. "I guess we won't be able to compare baby pictures after all, will we?"

"That's okay," Jana told her. Then she turned to Mrs. Barry and said happily, "If you don't have anyone in mind to give all those diapers to, I know someone who could use them."

Here's a preview of The Fabulous Five Super Edition #4, *Yearbook Memories*, coming soon to a bookstore near you.

"*I*'m certainly glad that Mr. Bell didn't call off the seventh-grade dinner dance because a few kids were drinking on the class trip," said Melanie. The Fabulous Five were sprawled in her room on Wednesday afternoon, after school had been dismissed for the year.

"Me, too," said Beth, "even though I don't have a date for the dance."

"You're going anyway, aren't you?" asked Jana.

Beth nodded. "Dekeisha doesn't have a date, and neither does Marcie Bee so we're all going together."

"Sit with us," said Katie. "And let's all get there early so we can get a big table."

"You know," Jana said wistfully, "I'm really going to miss being a seventh grader."

"I know what you mean," said Melanie. "It was a terrific year, and I have so many great memories. How could I ever forget all the trouble I got into over the seven tips for flirting or meeting Shane . . . and Igor?"

"I'd certainly like to forget when Randy was hit by a car and stayed in a coma for days," Jana said sadly.

Smiling softly, she added, "Thank goodness he's all right now."

"I'll always remember being on Teen Court and having to preside when Tony came before the court for illegally wearing an earring to school," said Katie, laughing.

"Yeah, and who would have ever dreamed that I'd get to be on TV?" asked Beth, looking starry-eyed.

"Speaking of dreams, remember the slumber party when we dreamed we were each other?" cried Jana.

"How could we forget!" declared Katie, and everybody laughed.

"I guess the worst thing that happened was when Christie moved to England," said Beth.

"Right," said Melanie, "and now she's coming back, and we're all going to be together again."

"I'll bet lots more memories will come flooding back at the dinner dance when Mr. Bell announces the awards and gives out the yearbooks," said Jana.

And that's exactly what will happen. Join The Fabulous Five in a look back at some funny, poignant, and surprising moments in seventh grade at Wakeman Junior High in The Fabulous Five Super Edition #4, *Yearbook Memories*.

THE FABULOUS FIVE
IS CHANGING!

Don't miss FAB 5 FOREVER, a brand-new series about The Fabulous Five's adventures in eighth grade, when Wakeman Junior High becomes Wakeman Middle School. FAB 5 FOREVER is coming soon to a bookstore near you!

Here are the answers to trivia questions #31–35, which appeared in the back of The Fabulous Five #31, *The Fabulous Five Together Again*.

#31 Where do students at Wacko Junior High stick their gum in the morning?
The gum tree.

#32 In book #7, *The Kissing Disaster*, what does Melanie's biology class dissect?
A cow's eyeball.

#33 What is Funny Hawthorne's real name?
Karen Janelle Hawthorne.

#34 In book #29, *Melanie Edwards, Super Kisser*, which student from Wakeman gets kissed by one of the members of The New Generation?
Kimm Taylor.

#35 In book #27, *The Scapegoat*, which of Christie Winchell's new friends from London is descended from royalty?
Conrad Farrell.

ABOUT THE AUTHOR

Betsy Haynes, the daughter of a former news-woman, began scribbling poetry and short stories as soon as she learned to write. A serious writing career, however, had to wait until after her marriage and the arrival of her two children. But that early practice must have paid off, for within three months Mrs. Haynes had sold her first story. In addition to a number of magazine short stories and the Taffy Sinclair series, Mrs. Haynes is also the author of *The Great Mom Swap* and its sequel, *The Great Boyfriend Trap*. She lives in Marco Island, Florida, with her husband, who is also an author.

From Bantam-Skylark Books

IT'S

From Betsy Haynes, the bestselling author of the Taffy Sinclair books, comes THE FABULOUS FIVE. Follow the adventures of Jana Morgan and the rest of THE FABULOUS FIVE in Wakeman Jr. High.

☐	SEVENTH-GRADE RUMORS (Book #1)	15625-X	$2.95
☐	THE TROUBLE WITH FLIRTING (Book #2)	15633-0	$2.95
☐	THE POPULARITY TRAP (Book #3)	15634-9	$2.95
☐	HER HONOR, KATIE SHANNON (Book #4)	15640-3	$2.95
☐	THE BRAGGING WAR (Book #5)	15651-9	$2.75
☐	THE PARENT GAME (Book #6)	15670-5	$2.75
☐	THE KISSING DISASTER (Book #7)	15710-8	$2.75
☐	THE RUNAWAY CRISIS (Book #8)	15719-1	$2.75
☐	THE BOYFRIEND DILEMMA (Book #9)	15720-5	$2.75
☐	PLAYING THE PART (Book #10)	15745-0	$2.75
☐	HIT AND RUN (Book #11)	15746-9	$2.75
☐	KATIE'S DATING TIPS (Book #12)	15748-5	$2.75
☐	THE CHRISTMAS COUNTDOWN (Book #13)	15756-6	$2.75
☐	SEVENTH-GRADE MENACE (Book #14)	15763-9	$2.75
☐	MELANIE'S IDENTITY CRISIS (Book #15)	15775-2	$2.75
☐	THE HOT-LINE EMERGENCY (Book #16)	15781-7	$2.99
☐	CELEBRITY AUCTION (Book #17)	15784-1	$2.75
☐	TEEN TAXI (Book #18)	15794-9	$2.75
☐	THE BOYS-ONLY CLUB (Book #19)	15809-0	$2.95
☐	THE WITCHES OF WAKEMAN (Book #20)	15830-9	$2.75
☐	JANA TO THE RESCUE (Book #21)	15840-6	$2.75
☐	MELANIE'S VALENTINE (Book #22)	15845-7	$2.95
☐	MALL MANIA (Book #23)	15852-X	$2.95
☐	THE GREAT TV TURNOFF (Book #24)	15861-7	$2.95
☐	THE FABULOUS FIVE MINUS ONE (Book #25)	15867-8	$2.99
☐	LAURA'S SECRET (Book #26)	15871-6	$2.99
☐	THE SCAPEGOAT (Book #27)	15872-4	$2.99
☐	BREAKING UP (Book #28)	15873-2	$2.99
☐	MELANIE EDWARDS, SUPER KISSER (Book #29)	15874-0	$2.99
☐	SIBLING RIVALRY (Book #30)	15875-9	$2.99
☐	THE FABULOUS FIVE TOGETHER AGAIN (Book #31)	15968-2	$2.99
☐	SUPER EDITION #1 THE FABULOUS FIVE IN TROUBLE	15814-7	$2.95
☐	SUPER EDITION #2 CARIBBEAN ADVENTURE	15831-7	$2.95

Buy them at your local bookstore or use this page to order:

Taffy Sinclair is perfectly gorgeous and totally stuck-up. Ask her rival Jana Morgan or anyone else in the sixth grade of Mark Twain Elementary. Once you meet Taffy, life will **never** be the same.

Don't Miss Any of the Terrific Taffy Sinclair Titles from Betsy Haynes!

☐ 15819-8 **TAFFY GOES TO HOLLYWOOD** $2.95

☐ 15607-1 **THE TRUTH ABOUT TAFFY SINCLAIR** $3.25

☐ 15645-4 **TAFFY SINCLAIR STRIKES AGAIN** $2.99

☐ 15647-0 **TAFFY SINCLAIR, QUEEN OF THE SOAPS** $3.25

☐ 15877-5 **NOBODY LIKES TAFFY SINCLAIR** $2.99

Follow the adventures of Jana and the rest of her friends in **THE FABULOUS FIVE** by Betsy Haynes.